Our
Writers In The North

TERMS AND CONDITIONS

R.C. Bagley

First published in Great Britain by Richard Bagley in conjunction with

Charlie Pearson and Our Writers In The North in 2019.

Cover Design by Charlie Pearson

To Wendy,

My Soulmate.

CHAPTER ONE

Steven Reid sat patiently at the wheel of the white transit van, which he had parked up at the side of the deserted country road, his dark green eyes studied the narrow road which stretched out for miles ahead of him, he was calm and in control, his army training had prepared him well for such things and in the two decades he spent in the forces he had done and seen a lot more than what he was about to do today.

He stared in silence out of the windscreen at the long empty road ahead, he looked in the rear-view mirror at the long empty road which stretched for miles behind him and he looked at the thick overgrown forest on either side that provided adequate cover for what he had planned. The weather also helped, it was windy with a chill in the air and the risk of rain had kept people away from what in the summer months was a busy country road, today though its exactly as Reid had wanted it to be, quiet and deserted.

As he sat waiting he ran his fingers through his neatly cut greying hair then folded his muscular tattooed arms and went through in his mind what he needed to do, he knew that everything had to run like clockwork, but in the forefront of his mind was the reason why he was doing this.

He was fully aware of the amount of trouble he would get himself into by doing what he was about to do, but from his head to his heart he believed he had no other option, of course there would be an opposing argument but those opposed to his plan haven't been through what he had, so his attitude to anyone who is opposed, they can go and screw themselves as far as he was concerned.

After forty minutes had passed, Reid saw in his mirror the vehicle he was waiting for. A white prison van was in the distance, from where he was parked he estimated that the prison van would be passing him in less than two minutes, he had done that exact journey dozens of times in preparation for today, he had thought of everything and covered nearly every eventuality.

He started the engine to the transit and pulled it across both lanes and completely blocked off the road, he then switched off the engine took the keys from the ignition and got out of the van, he ran over to the forest carrying his six-foot two-inch, muscular frame across the road quickly and positioned himself behind a tree, his dark clothing and the ski mask he calmly slipped over his head, making him difficult to locate. He remained out of sight, as he did so he pulled out a hand gun from his belt line and waited.

The prison van had two officers on board, one at the wheel and another locked in the back with the prisoners who were housed in their tiny cells throughout the journey to jail.

As the prison van approached the driver noticed the transit blocking their way, he eased of the gas and reached out to a panel of buttons situated on the dash board to his left and pressed the intercom button, the escort officer, sitting comfortably in his black high-backed captains seat in the rear of the vehicle, readjusted his position from resting to working and put on the headset, when he saw the intercom light was beeping.

"Is there a problem Pete"? He enquired, his visibility hindered by the almost pointless, twelve-inch square, side window he has to look out of. So, he had to rely on his driver to relay information to him. "There's a van blocking the road, and no sign of a driver" Pete replied, his voice sounding amplified by the radio.

The prison van drew to a halt, as the engine ticked over and made that loud chugging noise diesel engines do, both men pondered on the situation "so what's happening"? Asked Phil the escort officer, the side of his face pressed up against the thick plastic window, attempting to see. "I can't see the driver anywhere, the doors open but no sign of anyone" Pete replied, fully scanning the area from his more suitable vantage point.

He looked for less than a minute then came to a decision, "I'm going to get out and have a look, we can't wait here all day" he said, his northern accent prominent "we have to get to the prison before five and we still have eight miles to go" he pointed out.

Phil listened in on the headset, his head shaking left to right showing his disapproval “No, no, I wouldn’t do that mate, just call it in, you know you’re not meant to leave the vehicle” he replied. Phil was the cautious type, who did everything by the book, anyone who worked with him knew this and were tired of this.

Pete gave out an exasperated moan, the kind you could get away with if done to close friends “we’re hardly transporting a super grass or a top-ranking crime lord, we have a couple of burglars a car thief and some minor drug dealers, I don’t think anyone is planning on breaking anybody out, plus I need a piss” Pete replied almost in one breath, taking off his seat belt and turning off the wagons engine as he did.

It fell eerily quiet when the engine was stopped, the sound of complete silence seemed to fall heavily all around. From the safety of the cab, Pete had another quicker scan of the area, sensing himself how quiet it had become. It lasted just a moment when it was shattered by the sound of Pete's driver door creaking open.

With Phil trying to see through the side window and not having much luck, Pete exited the vehicle and slowly walked towards the transit, taking a couple of glances to his left then to his right as he approached the van. With the sound of the gravel road crunching beneath his every step and the sandy coloured dust collecting onto his polished boots.

He reached the driver's side of the vehicle, since the door was open he looked inside, he had no idea what he was looking for, but he noticed there was no keys in the ignition, and no theft damage either. Pete raised his head to look over the seat into the back and saw that it was empty. He walked to the front of the van and made his way to the passenger side, expecting to see an unconscious driver when he got there but he didn't see anyone.

Pete thought for a while on what best to do, it was obvious to him that the van needed pushing out of the way, but he would need Phil's help for that. He began to walk back to the prison van looking up to the sky, checking on the chances of them missing the approaching rain fall.

Reid however was watching every move he made, quietly and out of sight on the very edge of the forest. He had been waiting for Pete to start walking back to the prison van, knowing that he would have too, to talk to his colleague, he readied himself and allowed himself a small grin, his arrogance turned to surprise though, he was expecting the officer to relay any info via the intercom, he was then going to grab Pete and hold him at gun point, forcing the man inside to unlock the rear door, but Reid watched on as Pete went straight to the side door and began to unlock it to speak to Phil, asking him to help push the van out of the way.

Pete studied his hand as it slowly turned the key in the lock, he was expecting another lecture on the rules, he had a vision of Phil standing at the door, with rule book in hand, quoting from it that “the side door should only be opened when in the secure loading area of a court or police station” But Pete needed Phil’s help, there was no sign of anyone around and Pete didn’t worry about the rules as much as Phil, so he made the decision as he walked the dozen or so steps back to his van, to open Phil’s door.

The turning of the key was done in slow motion for Reid, he had come up onto his haunches and positioned his body like that of an athlete at the start line of a sprint race. With his breath held he waited for the click that would tell him the door was open.

Within the silence, Reid could hear perfectly clearly, and he recognised it when it came, with very quick reactions, he broke cover and sprinted out of the forest like he had been propelled out of the blocks, his clothing pressed against his torso as the wind resistance pushed against him.

His powerful legs helped him cover the twenty or so meters within a couple of seconds. And with the ease of a pro, he over powered his man, before Pete had even spotted him, pressing him face first against the side of the van, and sticking the pistol against Pete's head, "don't you fucking move you bastard" Reid shouted, Pete froze, for a split second lots of things went through his mind, was this some sort of prank? Was it for real?

Or had this gunman got the wrong van, because no one of any significance was on board. Deciding that the best thing to do was to comply with Reid's demands, after all, he didn't earn anywhere near enough to give his life or attempt any heroics.

Pete made a point of letting Reid know "Alright, take it easy, I'm going to do whatever you ask" he instructed, his voice shaking, Reid kept a tight grip, and spun Pete around, taking one step back Reid raised his arm and aimed the gun at his head, Pete pressed himself against the van, as if he wished he could just melt through it and escape, his whole body filled with fear, he began to shake uncontrollably, wondering if this was his final moment.

"you know what I want" Reid said, wanting to keep speech down to a minimum, on shaky legs, Pete strode over to the door and flung it open to reveal a frightened Phil standing up, against his escort seat with his hands in the air.

Dropping the built-in steps of the vehicle, Reid ordered Pete to get on board and instructed both men to go to the back and to face away, he reached over and took a set of keys from Phil's belt, Reid then turned and walked slowly up and down

the van "which cell is holding Craig Chambers"? He asked authoritatively, before a reply could be given, some of the other prisoners on the van began to demonstrate their wish to be freed.

Screaming, shouting, cheering and banging on their cell doors, with the thrill of a chance of escaping whipping them up into a frenzy, that Reid had to ignore.

Amongst all the noise coming from the other cells, there was one cell which didn't have noise coming from it, in it sat a skinny, unshaven and weak looking man in his twenties, he sat quietly and was left wondering as to why he'd heard his name mentioned.

Reid immediately noticed the stillness coming from cell two, and approached the door, he peered through the reinforced window and stared at chambers, who stared back completely unawares at what was happening.

As Reid studied Chambers' face for a few seconds he was attempting to block out the noise coming from the other cells, but there was One voice that could be heard over that of the other prisoners, it seemed to be transmitting on a different frequency and just stuck out to Reid within the crowd.

“Hey mate, unlock my door, let me out next and you can leave, I’ll unlock the others” pleaded the man in the cell directly opposite to the one Chambers was housed in.

His high voice along with the broad Liverpool accent echoing in Reid’s ears. He simply ignored the request and focussed his attention on Chambers, he recognised him from the court case, he looked deep into his eyes, staring right through him, which unsettled Chambers slightly. Chambers didn’t know him, and was confused to why he was being sprung from jail.

“Who are you”? he asked, “never mind” replied Reid as he unlocked the cell door, he took hold of Chambers’ arm and pulled him from the cell, “there is a white van outside, go and get in the back of it, lie down and wait for me” Reid instructed.

He spoke quickly at times, usually when under pressure. This was because his brain operated quickly, and this plan meant that he was working against the clock, so he had to remain in control and keep things running smooth. Chambers grabbed this opportunity with both hands, and left the prison van quickly, making his way to the white transit.

Reid looked at the two officers who still had their backs turned, “you two can turn around now” he said, both men did so and then complied with everything they were told to do.

Reid ordered the two guards into the cell that chambers had just vacated, it was a tight squeeze and after closing the door and locking both men inside, Reid’s attention was drawn to the prisoner in the opposite cell, who's voice was now becoming an annoyance to Reid.

The young prisoner's pleas to be freed had gone on and on, when some others had given up, "please mate, please, just unlock the door" he said desperately, Reid turned his head to look at the tall skinny kid, he was in his late teens with acne and greasy limp brown hair.

they both shared eye contact for a few seconds, Reid could tell from his appearance that the kid was a drug addict, and his drug of choice was more likely heroin, armed with this knowledge, Reid knew that the kid would be suffering from withdrawal soon, "Are you rattling yet"? Reid asked, "a little, yeah" was the answer from the visibly agitated prisoner, his skin sweaty and he had the shakes slightly, these symptoms would only get steadily worse as time went on.

“What are you in for”? Enquired Reid, showing an interest. “just a few silly Burglaries” replied the prisoner, who’s voice had now become a little calmer, because of the one on one chat with the man who could give him freedom “how long did you get”? Reid asked inquisitively, “Three years” replied the kid, his face showing the desperation at wanting to be freed.

Reid raised his left hand showing his index finger to the prisoner, who took this as him being told to wait for a second, Reid then turned to the two officers locked in the small cell, “you won’t be in here for long, I reckon someone will be along soon to let you out” he said reassuringly.

The uncertainty of this plan, didn’t work for Pete “I’m really going to need a piss sir” he said with a sense of desperation in his voice, which would grow bigger as time moved on. It had little effect on Reid however.

Holding onto his crotch, to stop himself from peeing his pants, Pete attempted to reach out to Reid "can I just go outside now? once I'm finished ill come straight back in I promise" Pleaded Pete, getting progressively more desperate.

Reid paused for a brief moment, considering Pete's idea "request denied, looks like there is a possibility that it's going to get messy in there" Reid pointed out in an uncaring manner, Reid then turned to face the kid opposite, whose eyes lit up in anticipation of being freed, "Be a man and do the time, then change your ways when you get out" said Reid, he then turned and walked towards the exit and left the vehicle, "Fuck you man" shouted the kid, unable to deal with the frustration and anger, "I hope when you're caught they put you in the same cell as me, I'll smash your skull in you prick" he carried on, his voice getting louder to ensure Reid would hear as he disappeared from view and walked to his transit van.

As Reid approached the van and with the voice of the kid being heard in the background, Reid noticed that Chambers was sitting proudly in the passenger seat, Reid reacted to this with sigh of disbelief and annoyance, he quickly walked around to the near side of the van and opened the door looking at Chambers, “I said to get in the back” Reid said exasperated, “its covered in shit, I’m not lying in that” replied Chambers.

The van was over a decade old, and dented in parts and rusty in others, Reid had stolen it a week previously when it was parked up on the side of the road one night, for whatever purpose it was being used, it had made the rear of the vehicle a mess, with oil, dried mud and grease covering the floor.

Chambers' inability to follow instructions was holding things up and Reid never had time to argue, he was against the clock, the fact Chambers had ignored his instructions, coupled with the loud voice of the prisoner inside the prison van verbally attacking Reid was starting to agitate him.

So, with the vile insults and threats, that where now being directed to Reid's parents, brothers, sisters and anyone that

the young burglar hoped would get a reaction, ringing in his ears, Reid told Chambers one last time to get into the back of the van, Chambers however, remained stubborn "I'm alright in this seat" he replied, "shouldn't we be thinking about getting out of here?" he asked like he was running the show.

It wasn't as if he was trying to avoid hurting Chambers, it was quite the opposite, he was looking for an excuse to and he'd just found one, with one very fast and immensely powerful right hook, Reid struck Chambers on his temple, it was as if someone had turned out the lights for Chambers, being knocked unconscious within a fraction of a second after the punch was thrown and landed, in one fluid motion, as chambers' body fell limp, Reid grabbed his legs and lifted them over his head, tipping him over the seat, he fell in a heap onto the filthy floor of the van.

Reid slammed the van door and walked back towards the driver's seat, the voice of the kid could still be heard, since the other things he'd shouted hadn't worked, he was attempting to taunt Reid with insults about his wife "I'll put her in a hole, you don't know who you're messing with, you dickhead" shouted the young addict in anger, Reid, by now, was wasting

time that he didn't have, and he was becoming irate at this scouse big mouth.

Before Reid climbed into the van he pulled out the pistol from his belt line and fired two shots in quick succession into the side of the van, the bullets entered the cell where the kid was ranting from and went straight through the body work, one bullet embedding itself into the solid hard plastic seat and the other going straight through the door ricocheting from the impact and penetrating the floor, suddenly silence fell, the kid was stunned and shaken, he knew those bullets could have easily hit him and it was either luck that they didn't or that Reid was a crack shot, whichever it was he knew he was lucky to be still alive or at least uninjured, the only sound left to be heard was that of the van door slamming shut, the engine starting and the van driving away quickly.

A few miles further down the road Reid pulled into a lay-by, he stopped the van, pulled on the hand brake and climbed from his seat into the back where chambers was laying, by now he was beginning to come around, he was moaning slightly as he began to feel the throbbing pain in his head caused by the punch.

Reid flipped Chambers over onto his front and began to tie his hands together using black plastic cable ties; they were the tool of a professional, very light and thin so you could carry dozens of them with you at any one time and very strong, once they were fastened to your wrists you were not getting out of them. He fastened them tightly, so his skin protruded over them, and he fastened his legs in the same manner then turned him over onto his back and stared at Chambers.

Chambers, who was now fully conscious, was petrified and it showed in his voice "who are you, What are you going to do with me"? he asked, his voice shaking, Reid didn't answer, he looked deep into the eyes of Chambers which filled with puzzlement at what was happening, "please, I'm nobody, I've done nothing to you, please don't kill me" he pleaded, Reid grabbed hold of the scruff of Chambers' neck with both hands and lifted his shaking torso up off the van floor and towards himself, his face just inches away from Chambers, "I'm not going to kill you, I need you alive for now" Reid said as he suddenly let go of him, making Chambers crash to the floor, the back of his head feeling the impact as his body landed.

"Why are you doing this to me"? Asked Chambers, as he watched Reid retrieve a black sports bag from under the driver's seat "You ask to many questions, you'll find out all in good time" came the reply, "now listen carefully, I'm going to gag and blindfold you" explained Reid as he pulled a black hood and a large roll of silver coloured duct tape from the bag, "if you make any noise what so ever at any point, I promise I'll kill you very slowly so you will feel every bit of the pain and agony that I'll put upon you, do you understand"? Chambers didn't speak, he just nodded in reply, he was cold, dirty, in pain and frightened and he had no idea why he was being held captive.

As Reid placed a strip of tape over Chambers' mouth and a black pillow case over his head, Chambers' body fell limp, He suffered with claustrophobia so as soon as the hood was placed over his head the palpitations started.

The hood restricted his breathing and now with his hands tied also, he felt helpless and weak, add that to the fear he was experiencing due to this stranger holding him captive and it took all of his self-control to try and remain calm.

"Relax and try and get comfortable, you can breathe fine through the hood, so control your breath" instructed Reid, noticing the beads of sweat running down the forehead of Chambers, he had no compassion for this man, however it would make things easier if Chambers was quiet and complying rather than panicking which is why he offered the few words of advice before climbing back into the driver's seat and driving off again.

Getting comfortable wasn't an easy thing to do, the floor was dirty, cold and hard, and the motion of the van due to the fast erratic driving of Reid threw Chambers around quite a lot, Chambers could do nothing else other than just lay there, fighting to remain in control of himself plus wondering what was in store for him and why he had been taken, these where questions that he hoped would be answered in a few hours' time.

CHAPTER TWO

The daylight had turned into night, the temperature had dropped and the sight of the large flames on the log fire inside the cosy lounge area of the quaint country pub looked very inviting to Reid, who was standing in the car park at the rear of the pub, he had positioned himself in some of the large bushes near to the entrance, which enabled him to see into the lounge through the window, he was now wearing a thick black winter jacket to protect him from the cold with the collars up and a black scarf round his neck and black gloves.

The pub was only small but very comfortable with big comfy high-backed leather chairs and matching sofas, it had thick red carpets and the bar was made from oak which had been sanded smooth and varnished. It had a variety of different beers on offer to its customers who mainly consisted of the locals of the small village who all knew each other by first name.

The pub wasn't particularly busy this night, it was nearly a quarter to ten and it had about a dozen people inside, who were scattered around, a small group of elderly gentlemen

playing dominoes, a group of younger men playing darts and a few more elderly men sat by the fire talking.

It was one of the men sat near the fire that Reid was interested in, a tall man in his late sixties, with thinning grey hair and tanned skin, he was dressed in casual trousers and a thick plain jumper, his rain coat, along with others, was hanging on the coat stand near to the door.

On the table in front of him was a half-drunk pint of Guinness, he was a popular man who held court with the group of men in his company, they found him to be interesting and hung on his every word no matter what the subject was, he seemed to be an authority on most things.

Some of the people in the pub referred to him by name, which was 'Brian Pengilly' and others, identified him by the job he did and simply called him 'Judge'. Reid was a master planner, he had watched Pengilly for weeks, noting down his movements, he knew what time he woke in the morning, what time he set off for work, what time he returned home on an evening, when and where he walks his dogs with his wife and he knew that

Pengilly drank in his local pub every Friday evening from eight o' clock till ten, then he would walk the half mile back through the quiet and affluent village to his large detached cottage which was over two hundred years old. It was good for Reid that Pengilly was a creature of habit and that he stuck to the same routine as if it was a ritual.

As the fine drizzle started to come down and a thin veil of fog began to set in, Reid watched patiently as the three dart players put on their coats and walked from the bar and out into the car park, they congregated near some picnic tables just near the exit door and each lit up a cigarette, these three were not regulars and where from out of town, they were in their late twenties and made some of the locals of the pub feel a little uneasy with their loud behaviour.

Reid monitored Pengilly and saw him take another drink of his pint leaving only one mouthful left, He knew that the presence of the three men was not ideal, it could become problem, but he hoped that they would finish their smokes and return to the pub before Pengilly left the premises.

As he kept a close eye on the Judge, he remained hidden in the bushes and deathly quiet, the bushes where only a few feet away from where the men were standing, and any sound might alert them of his presence.

As he waited, wet and feeling the cold, Reid overheard one of the men tell his friends that he needed to go to the toilet, one of the men offered to hold onto his cigarette while he went inside to use the gents, this offer was declined, and the man decided it was quiet enough to just relieve himself in the bushes, unaware that Reid was hiding in them.

The man, who was of similar height to Reid but was much bigger in build made his way to the bushes, with his cigarette in his lips, he undid his fly and began to urinate into the bushes not realising that he was urinating on Reid who remained motionless and in the darkness.

When the man's eyes had adjusted to the dark, he jumped back when he noticed the dark figure of Reid in the bushes and let out an involuntary yelp, "what the fuck are you doing?" He said loudly, alerting his friends who joined the man at the

bushes, Reid, knowing his cover was blown, slowly stepped out from the bushes and faced the three men, in a matter of seconds he had the situation evaluated and should things turn nasty he had his escape plan prepared.

The other two men were not as big as their friend, they were both of average height but where above average build, one of the men had a boxer's nose so Reid had worked out that he was used to taking a punch and used to throwing one too.

The demeanour of the three was becoming aggressive, "answer him" instructed the boxer, "I've just pissed all over him" said the first man, Reid never said a word and went to walk away but was stopped by the first man who stood in his way, the man was just inches away from Reid and stood square on to him like two prize fighters facing off. The man, privately in his mind, compared his build to that of Reid, he noted that he was bigger, and along with his two pals by his side, it gave him the confidence to intimidate Reid.

the other two men took up positions either side of Reid, Reid recognised the danger of having these three men surrounding him and took a quick look at Pengilly through the window, he saw that he was placing his empty glass onto the bar and made his way over to the rack to collect his coat.

He had a matter of seconds if he was going to achieve his objective, but the three men where giving him a problem that he didn't need, so he attempted to engage with them, hoping that he could talk his way out of this situation.

He had been in much trickier situations than this in the past, sometimes lives where on the line, but he simply never had time for this one and he needed to end it straight away before it escalated into something else.

"Let's leave it lads, there's no need for any trouble" explained Reid who went to walk past the first man, but again his path was blocked, “what where you doing in the bushes pervert”? said the man standing his ground, “waiting for a young female to attack and rape probably” said the boxer whose stance had now become one of a man preparing for a fight, the other two had also blown themselves up to make themselves look bigger and nastier.

Reid recognised that the three men where in fight mode, the expressions on their faces and the way they were standing told him that. He noticed, while staring through the window of the lounge, that Pengilly had put on his coat and was saying good evening to some of the regulars, suddenly and without warning the first man slapped Reid’s face, he had taken exception to Reid’s attention being on what was going on in the pub, rather than what was happening in the car park “stop looking over there and answer the fucking question” Reid’s face was stinging by the slap, and his cheek was reddened, he could feel the anger building up inside which it often did whenever another man laid their hands on him.

Within a micro second of the slap contacting Reid's face and with cat like reflexes, Reid smashed his forehead onto the nose of the man who had slapped him, breaking it instantly, the man dropped to the floor, with thick dark red blood spilling down his face and onto his clothing, the head-butt was just a natural reaction, done without thought, as it was Reid's normal way to defend himself, using whichever method needed at the time.

Before the other two could react, Reid connected with a right hook to the jaw of the boxer, who stumbled back a few steps, giving Reid a vital few seconds to deal with the third man. Planting his feet and swinging from his waist he swung his big left fist into the face of man number three, who hadn't spoke during the short verbal exchange between the four.

As the punch connected it made a cracking sound as Reid's knuckles collided with the jaw bone of the man who fell to the floor like a tree being felled in a forest, he was unconscious before his body made impact with the ground.

The boxer had regained his balance and threw a left hook of his own which Reid had anticipated and managed to duck underneath the powerful shot, Reid's body twisted in such a way that it enabled him to throw a right uppercut as he came back up from dodging the left hook, the punch had started from his knees and by the time it connected with the chin of the boxer it was travelling so fast and so powerfully it carried on past the target, lifting the boxer off his feet, causing him to land in a heap on the wet concrete floor, leaving him staring up at the night sky, his brain scrambled from the ferocity of the single punch.

Within a matter of a few seconds, Reid, who was outnumbered and outsized by the three men, had left them laid out on the ground, with each one nursing a wound of some sort, Immediately Reid looked towards the pub, He saw that Pengilly was coming out through the main entrance as he normally does, Reid ran to his van which was parked just near the car park exit, and placed himself out of sight behind it, he could see both doors from his viewpoint, which were adjacent to each other but where about twenty-five meters apart.

As he watched for Pengilly, Reid could also see that the first man he'd hit with the head-butt was slowly picking himself up off the floor, his right hand covering his nose causing blood to drip through his fingers and onto the floor.

As the judge, who was completely unaware of the injured three, left the pub and slowly made his way across the car park he stopped and turned around when he heard a moaning sound coming from the smoking area, through the darkness and as his eyes adjusted he could see the figure of a man, unsteady on his feet, and he looked to be attending to another man who was laid on the floor, “Is everything alright over there”? shouted the judge, before he could get an answer Reid quickly

approached him from behind and forcefully placed a black hood over his head, he then grabbed both elderly man’s arms and placed them up his back, pushing them upwards towards his shoulder blades, making the judge go onto his tiptoes, he cried out in pain as Read quickly walked him the few meters to where his van was waiting, there was no resistance from Pengilly as Reid was too strong, too fast and too skilful for elderly Judge.

“You’re breaking my arms” shouted Pengilly in obvious pain, Reid never reacted, instead, upon reaching the van he opened up one of the back doors and pushed the judge inside, by now two of the men who had the altercation with Reid where back on their feet, both with blood streaming down their faces they had witnessed what was happening on the opposite side of the car park, not wanting to take another beating from Reid they both decided to run back into the pub and alert the people inside.

As they did so, Reid was in the back of the van and had the judge lying face down, still with the hood over his head, next to him was the motionless and silent figure of Chambers who had been there since he was taken earlier that afternoon. Reid

fastened Pengilly's hands together behind his back using the same method he'd used earlier on Chambers, he then bent forward and whispered in his ear "if you make one sound, I'll kill your family, your friends and then I'll kill you" The next thing Pengilly heard was the sound of Reid exiting the van and slamming the door, he had been a judge for over thirty years and had dealt with some of the nastiest and vicious criminals around, he was shaking with fear, his wife and family ran through his head, he took Reid's threat seriously and remained silent even though he was certain that Reid was now outside the van.

He tried to work out what was going on, he immediately thought that this man was someone He had sent down for some considerable years and this was revenge, he knew that he would find out eventually so decided for the safety of himself and his family that he would obey everything that was said to him Reid by now was sitting in the driver's seat of the van, he turned the key in the ignition, starting the engine; he saw a group of the pubs drinkers joined by two of the three men he had assaulted flow out of the pub and into the car park, with one of his victims indicating to the group to where Reid was.

Reid was certain that the police had been called, and he had to get out of there before they turned up. As he put the van into gear and lowered the hand break he saw a few of the locals cautiously walk towards him.

Stepping on the gas he set off with the vans wheels screeching, he drove straight towards the few men who each jumped out of the way of the speeding van, Reid hadn't switched on the vans headlights as he wanted to make sure that any witnesses had little idea to which direction he had gone, as he drove out of the car park and sped off along the high street he disappeared out of sight to the watching few who had ran towards the exit.

Phase two of the plan was complete both Pengilly and Chambers where tied up and silent in the back of the van in fear for their lives and Reid was about to put phase three into action.

CHAPTER THREE

Reid was parked up at the side of the road in an area that could pass for millionaire's row, each property was the size of a small mansion each with acres of land at the rear and a considerable size garden to the front. Large trees scattered around the land, big gates and long driveways with Aston Martins, Jaguars and BMW's parked upon them. The few dozen houses which stood on hundreds of acres of land where built within the last decade and very modern but built to have an old English theme to them coupled with environmentally friendly design, each roof was adorned with solar panelling and had grand entrance hallways, wide stairs and between five and seven bedrooms.

The one house in particular that Reid was interested in was no different to the others in terms of design and size and it stood in a large wooded area of land, Reid started the van and pulled up to the wide solid wooden gate, he got out of the van with engine running and opened up the gate which just had a simple catch on it and no locks, Reid drove slowly onto the driveway leaving the gate open, he approached the front of the

house, parking the van next to the brand-new Mercedes which sat there.

This house belonged to Oliver Bilton Russell, he was a successful barrister, early fifties, tall and slim, he played squash twice a week and enjoyed running through the forest that his house backed onto to keep in shape. He took great pride in his appearance, he wore expensive suits and heavy watches.

Unlike the other high court barristers that he knew, Bilton Russell wasn't grey and balding with a paunch and yellow teeth, He was envied by most of his male colleagues.

He also knew his worth and knew what he had going for him, the fact that he was handsome, rich and successful made him a man who received a lot of attention from women he met. And he was fully aware, and so was everyone else in the profession, that he was a damn good barrister, with only the wealthy and sometimes famous using his services to get them out of any sticky situation, he loved his life, and the fact that he came from a very wealthy and privileged background.

Today however Bilton Russell was going to be thrown into a certain set of circumstances that he had never encountered before. This Saturday morning had started like any other, Bilton Russell had been for an early morning run, a quick three miles around the woods that surrounded his home and he had showered in his spacious shower and dressed in casual jeans and T shirt and settled down in the large light modern living room with the guardian newspaper and began to enjoy his weekend.

His wife of some twenty years was busy cooking in the huge kitchen, as well as making a pot of tea for her and her husband to sit and enjoy, she was five years older than Russell and everything about her was fake, from her dyed hair, her filled lips, false boobs, long painted finger nails and lipo sucked body, she had leathery dark tanned skin and was desperately trying to hold onto the beauty and youth that she once had decades earlier.

As both parties busied themselves in the house, Reid had opened the back of the van and made sure the doors remained open, he pulled a ski mask from his coat pocket and pulled it over his head, with his right hand he pulled a hand gun from his belt line and confidently walked to the large black glossy door of Russell's house and knocked hard three times then waited with his hands and the gun behind his back.

Hearing the knock on the door Russell looked up from his newspaper, expecting to see his wife walk by the door and down the hallway to answer it, he waited a few seconds and when a second knock came he folded his paper placed it onto the coffee table in front of him and rose to answer the door.

As he strode down the corridor he could make out the figure of a man dressed in black through the panels of patterned glass that decorated both sides of the large door, he muttered to himself as he reached out for the handle "more bloody home shopping deliveries no doubt" as he pulled the door open he was met with the cold metal barrel of the hand gun pressing against his forehead, Reid walked forward pushing the gun into Russell forcing him to take a few steps back, His mind froze for a second, not knowing what to do or say, Reid pushed him back against the wall in the hallway, With the gun still pointing at his head Russell attempted to control the situation "Okay, take it easy, we have no cash in the house

but there is lots of expensive jewellery upstairs" he said as calmly as he could manage.

Reid moved the gun from his forehead, and placed it against his temple, he leant forward and whispered into the ear of Russell "where's the wife Oliver"? asked Reid, Russell was puzzled at how Reid knew his name, he answered cautiously "she's in the kitchen" Reid listened and could hear the noises of Mrs Bilton Russell busy working in the kitchen which was situated at the end of the long hallway, he ordered Oliver to call her, with a nervous gulp and clearing his throat he called for his wife and both waited as the noise of work suddenly stopped and was replaced with the footsteps of Mrs Bilton Russell walking from the kitchen to where Reid was holding her husband against the wall with a gun against his head.

As she made her way into the hallway her attention, at first, was centred on checking her hands where free of any dirt but as she slowly lifted her head whilst she walked she caught sight of her husband at gun point, his face showed his fear and the sight of Reid dressed in black with a menacing stare peering out from behind the ski mask was enough to scare anyone.

Upon seeing and then comprehending the situation Mrs Bilton Russell gave out a startled scream, she froze to the spot at the sight of a hooded Reid holding a gun against her husband's head; she visibly began to shake with fear "Calm down, no one is going to be harmed if you do exactly as I ask" Reid said slowly and reassuringly, he then instructed her to unlock the door to the cellar, the entrance of which was in the hallway they were standing in.

He watched in silence as she shakily took the keys from a cabinet in the living room and wandered back out and unlocked the wooden door, she opened it to reveal a set of sturdy wooden stairs that led down into the cellar.

Reid positioned Russell at the top of the stairs, placed the gun under his chin and with his left arm he retrieved a folded piece of paper from his trouser pocket "you're free to go" he said handing her the paper, Mrs Bilton Russell nervously took hold of the paper but didn't move, she remained motionless, frozen to the spot, she wanted to move, she wanted to run out of there but her legs weren't getting the message her brain was sending out "Mrs Bilton Russell" Reid said slightly more loudly, but still he received no reply, Reid then shouted it

like an order to a soldier "MRS BILTON RUSSELL" he bellowed in his best drill sergeants voice, she jumped suddenly, the severity of the situation dawning on her, Reid continued "give that piece of paper to the police when they arrive" he then turned his new hostage around so he faced the cellar stairs and instructed him to walk down them, as he did so he turned to Mrs Bilton Russell one more time, she was trembling like a frightened animal, Reid pulled the ski mask from his head and glared at her "get the fuck out" he said in a menacing tone "NOW" he shouted at her, making her turn and run out of the house screaming.

Reid forced his captive down the fourteen stairs to the cellar. The cellar was the same size as the square footage of the entire house, it had been turned into two separate areas, one area which ran directly under the kitchen and hallway of the house and opposite the staircase was being used as a work shop, there were several tool boxes standing on top of each other and other tools such as spanners and screw driver sets hung up on the wall in size order, there was a seven-foot-long and very strong work bench with a vice attached to one end.

The bench and vice were covered in saw dust and metal filings, left over from jobs that had been carried out there in the past, On the other side of the cellar, Russell had turned it into his winery, a hobby that he adored, he had six wooden racks adjacent to each other which stood about six-foot-high, each wine rack held about ten bottles of wine per row and had six rows each so a full rack would hold sixty bottles, Upon these racks laid over three hundred bottles of wine, most of which were thick with dust, and probably hadn't been moved or even touched for years, they originated from all over the globe, every bottle was very expensive with some being worth several thousands and others being in the region of tens of thousands of pounds each, this wasn't the type of wine a person drank but more collected as an investment.

Reid opened three folding chairs which he had found occupying one corner of the cellar along with some old camping equipment which looked like it hadn't been used in years and placed them behind the work bench facing the stairs, keeping the gun trained on his scared and confused prisoner at all times. He forcefully manoeuvred Russell around and sat him down on the chair.

Instructing him to place his hands palm down on the bench, as he did so Reid produced a drill from a tool box, to the astonishment to Russell who wondered how he knew exactly where to find such an item, and proceeded to drill a single hole on either side of Russell's wrists, after doing this Reid then threaded a black plastic cable tie through the holes and over a bewildered Russell's wrists, he fastened the cable tie at both ends then pulled it tightly so it secured his hands to the bench and he was unable to move sufficiently to escape.

Reid then took hold of Russel's hair pulling his head back violently "while you wonder how I seem to know exactly where things are, I’m going to bring in our other guests” Reid said, letting go of Russel and walking towards the stairs in a confident manner “it’s as if I’ve been down here dozens of times without you knowing” he said leaving Russell to ponder such a thing while Reid climbed the stairs and made his way outside to the van.

While looking at his two captives, laid in silence with their heads covered in the back of the van, Reid grabbed a leg of each man and dragged them from the van until they landed with a thud on the gravel floor, the judge letting out a gasp as the fall winded him, Reid then slammed both doors to the van and grabbing a leg each again he dragged the two scared men away from the van, the stones from the gravel driveway cutting into the body of both men as they were dragged along and into the house feet first.

He dropped hold of the legs and slammed the big black door shut, and locked the two strong chrome bolts on the door, using a knife he pulled from a sheath on his belt he cut the hands free of both men and instructed them to stand up and remove their hoods, both men did as requested but with nervous caution, they were then both told to walk down the stairs to the cellar, with neither man wanting to take the lead Reid began shoving both of them towards the cellar door where he followed them as they descended the stairs and took their place either side of the Barrister as instructed to do so by Reid.

At gunpoint Reid gave Pengilly step by step instructions on securing Chambers to the table in the same way he had done with Russell, he then fastened Pengilly to the table in the same fashion.

After satisfying himself that the three men where secured to the work bench and unable to get free he placed thick duct tape over the mouths of the three and then turned and ran up the stairs, taking two of the steps at a time, Reid burst out into the hallway and quickly unlocked the main door and out to the van where he picked up a bag from the passenger seat and returned to the house, he locked the door for a second time and trotted upstairs, going from room to room he checked that there were no open windows and that all the windows were locked and that there were no entry points anywhere.

After a short while Reid returned to the ground floor and made the same checks in all the rooms, in a few of the rooms such as the kitchen, the main sitting room and in the conservatory, he pulled from the bag an incendiary device, Reid had been an explosives expert in the army and had collected the correct ingredients and made the three devices at home in preparation for this plan, he activated all the devices and placed them down, out of sight in the corners of each selected room.

Satisfied that the house was secure, Reid went through the cellar door and locked it behind him, placing the key in his pocket, He then walked down the stairs, taking each step deliberately slowly until he stood on the lower half of the stairs and stared at the three men who were now his prisoners, the three men, unable to speak because of the tape, just stared back at him, their eyes wide and each facial expression speaking a thousand words, nearly all of which represented fear, anguish and torment.

The room fell silent for a length of time that made it uncomfortable for the three hostages, Reid, who was deliberately not talking and just staring at his captives, knew how to build the pressure perfectly well, the sense of fear hanging in the air was palpable and all created by Reid, using interrogation tactics that the army had taught him so well.

In years gone by, he had gained information and knowledge from some tough and battle-hardened soldiers, mercenaries and terrorists, so he was confident that when the questions start to be asked, the answers won't be hard to come by.

He slowly walked down the last few stairs and wandered over to the three men and stood directly opposite them, he took the gun from his belt and placed it onto the table so it sat inches away from the three as if to taunt them, with their hands fastened to the table and their mouths taped shut Reid just observed their facial expressions for a while until he broke the silence "Now it begins gentlemen, you will all begin to understand what all this is about as this day goes on" With everything now done, that was another phase of the plan complete, and Reid felt satisfied and content, as he knew that at some point during the course of the day, that he would be getting the answers that he needed.

However, at this time, it was just a matter of waiting, Reid had no idea how long for, he never anticipated waiting for a very long time, but however long it was going to be, it was essential that he followed the plan and remained calm and in control throughout.

The three hostages, all sitting staring straight ahead, and trying to avoid eye contact with Reid, had several things running through their heads, the main common theme being, are they going to survive this, or will they be leaving the cellar in a body bag.

Reid knew that these kinds of thoughts would run through their minds, he was an expert and had been well trained, and he had done this kind of thing many times before, it was positive for Reid to have his hostages think things like that, as when it comes to question time, then they are more likely to tell him everything that he wants to know in a short space of time.

CHAPTER FOUR

Jo Tucker had come up the hard way; she was early forties, pretty, of slight build with shoulder length blonde hair and dark green eyes. It had taken her twenty years of policing to make the rank of inspector and along the way she faced a barrage of adversity, with sexism and bullying raising their ugly heads frequently.

She had a strong will and refused to let such things beat her, she had been passed over for promotion several times but never gave up, she just worked even harder, in the early days she wasn't the most popular officer on her shift, because of her drive and determination she often rubbed people up the wrong way, but it was only so she could fulfil her ambitions and what she believed was her full potential as a high-ranking police officer.

It had taken all the years of hard work and sacrifice and her willingness to muck in and get her hands dirty for her to finally reach the rank of inspector and gain the respect of her colleagues, she had also gained a reputation as a no-nonsense type of person, she was very clever and knew her job

inside out, her superiors knew that whatever task was in front of her it would be completed using her intelligence and experience and she always got her man, she had never let anyone slip through her fingers and she was proud of that fact.

It was two in the morning and Jo and a hand full of officers were sitting in the back of an unmarked police van, a girl in her late teens had been kidnapped whilst on her way home from work a few days previously, the unenviable task of making the ransom drop had fallen to Alan Harley the elder brother of the kidnapped girl and the location of the drop was a small car park at the only entrance to a large forest, popular with horse riders and dog walkers a few miles from the nearest town.

Jo was sitting on the wheel arch of the van, opposite Alan who was understandably nervous as his sister's life now rested on him making the drop without any mistakes, Jo knew that he wasn't happy about the police involvement, he was willing to just pay the hundred grand and not inform the authorities as requested by the kidnapper, but he was overruled by his parents, Jo could sense he was reluctant to go ahead with the

police covering the area so reached across and held both of his hands as she spoke "Look Alan, I completely understand how you are feeling" she said, "Do you"? Came the dismissive reply, this wasn't the first pep talk she had given and certainly wouldn't be the last, "yes I do, I've been in this job for two decades and I've lost count how many cases like this I've done" she replied in a calm tone.

Alan still wasn't convinced and pulled his hands away slowly "I still think we should have just paid the money without all this, its Laurens life at risk here" Jo looked deep into his eyes, and spoke softly and slowly in what was her trade mark manner, "why do you think kidnappers always say not to inform the police"? Alan didn't answer, so Jo carried on "it's because they know that if the police are involved they will be caught, now I'm not going to lie to you, sometimes, very rarely, things don't work out like we'd like them too, but in my personal experience I've always caught the kidnappers and always got the victim back safe and sound, and that is exactly what I intend to do now, and do you want to know how I know that"? Again, Alan was silent and just sat still and listened, Jo once again took hold of Alan's hands and carried on talking “it’s because I’m clever, I’m smarter than this guy, there hasn’t been a criminal yet who has out smarted me and trust me

when I say this, this guy is a chancer, nothing more, he thinks he’s got the perfect plan, well there is no such thing as the perfect plan.

He has picked a very dark and secluded forest for the drop, in the hope that he can use the night as cover, but that isn’t going work for him”, Jo paused for a short while to make sure Alan was following what she was saying, “I promise that I’ll have him in a cell before the sun is up and Lauren will be back at home with you and the rest of the family, safe and well, but I’m asking you to trust me” Alan remained silent and thought for a moment, deep down he knew that involving the police was the right thing to do and there was no chance of catching the kidnapper without them, But he had heard about operations going wrong and he was nervous for his sister's safety.

Jo sat looking at Alan, waiting for his reply, Alan sighed "Yes I'll trust you, but if my sister is hurt in any way, I'm holding you personally responsible" he replied, "I wouldn't expect it any other way" replied Jo whose demeanour suddenly changed; she switched from being calm to acting like she meant business, the whole vibe inside the van suddenly changed, the

electricity Jo was giving out affected everyone, now the hairs on people's arms where standing on end and hearts where beating fast, Jo was now at work, it was game on.

She looked at one of her officers "time check sergeant" she asked, the officer looked at his watch and replied, "Quarter past two" Jo Carried on with instructions "ok Alan, you need to be at the meeting point for half past, remember we're watching, you won't see us, just follow whatever he tells you to do and leave the rest to us, is that clear"? Alan simply nodded, then exited the van and climbed into his car which was parked next to it, Jo watched from the open back door of the van as Alan started the engine of the car, he unzipped the bag which sat on the passenger seat and checked the money inside, he then zipped it back up again and began to drive the few miles to meeting point.

The headlights of Alan's car cut through the fog as he slowly entered the car park, as he drove into it he could hear the sound of the gravel crushing under his wheels. The car park was in a horse shoe shape with one entrance and one exit, it was a well-used car park during the day and held about fifty cars, Alan parked the vehicle next to the pathway entrance to the forest and turned off his engine.

He sat for a moment and took a deep calming breath, he knew he was being watched, definitely by the police who were somewhere around and possibly by the kidnapper, he got out of the vehicle and looked deep into the darkness that surrounded him, it came as no surprise when all he could see was the pitch blackness of night and all he could hear was the blowing of the trees, the scurrying around of nocturnal animals, and the hooting of an owl.

As Alan stood there he heard nearby the sound of a ringing phone, he diverted his gaze towards the floor and it wasn’t long before he saw the glowing face of a mobile phone standing up against a small newly planted tree, approximately five meters from where Alan was standing.

Alan picked it up and with a quick glance of the flashing face he pressed the answer key “hello” he said in a quiet voice “introduce yourself please” came the reply in a gruff whisper, as if the owner of the voice was attempting to disguise it or

trying in some way to sound menacing, either way Alan just wanted his sister back safe so answered the question “my name is Alan, I’m Laurens brother” he said, there was a pause for a few seconds, long enough for Alan to wonder if the call was still connected “are you still there”? he asked, there was another pause and then the voice spoke again “Put your left arm in the air” was the instruction, Alan had made the decision that he was prepared to do whatever necessary to get his sister back home safe and sound, so raised his arm without hesitation.

Hidden within the thick foliage about thirty meters from Alan's position was a middle-aged man of stocky build, his face covered with camouflage paint of greens and shades of brown and wearing army fatigues, he silently watched Alan raise his arm through the night vision goggles mounted onto his head, raising the phone to his mouth he spoke to Alan "I can see you" he said in a theatrically scary voice.

Alan began to search the darkness again whilst the voice on the other end of the phone began to relay instructions. "I want you to get the bag and carry it along the pathway, keep

going until I tell you to stop" he said reverting back to the gruff whisper from before.

Without hesitation, Alan grabbed the bag from the seat and locked the car, he then began his walk along the path, every step was treacherous, even more so in the pitch darkness. The mud beneath his feet was soft and slippery, his Italian loafers were not ideal hiking boots and the ground was littered with rocks, fallen branches, tree stumps and horse dung.

As every step he made took him deeper and deeper into the forest, Alan thought he had never seen darkness like it when he was standing in the car park, but as he ventured along the narrow winding path he saw the night become visibly blacker than before, he was in blindness and he was scared, his senses where heightened already because of the circumstances which had him out after two in the morning, but he knew he was being watched by the kidnapper but had no clue what the kidnapper had planned for him, was he going to make it out of the forest uninjured or even alive.

Also, Alan didn't like the darkness, he could hear movement amongst the trees and bushes, he reassured himself that it was just animals like badgers and foxes, and he was there to get his sister back, so he concentrated on that thought and carried on.

With the bag slung over his shoulder, he walked with his arms stretched out in front of himself to help guide his way. He fell over a few times, he either slipped over on the mud or tripped over an object that he didn't see or know what it was, a couple of times upon falling down he dropped the mobile phone which resulted in him crawling around on all fours, feeling with his hands through the sloppy mud to find it.

The kidnapper, on one occasion, helped Alan locate the phone after he dropped it, by giving him directions to where the phone was lying on the ground, as he could clearly see it through his goggles, with simple left, right and straight forward directions, it helped Alan retrieve the phone.

Every move Alan made was witnessed by the kidnapper, who maintained a distance of over ten meters away at least, he

also managed to manoeuvre through the trees silently as he and Alan progressed through the forest "You should have brought a torch Alan" he said with a smirk, "I would have if I'd known I was going to be trekking through a forest" came the agitated reply.

Alan had been moving slowly along the winding pathway for about fifteen minutes under the watchful eye of the mystery voice on the other end of the phone; he decided to strike up a conversation with the voice "how many times have you done this"? He asked, there was a short pause then the kidnapper dismissed Alan's question and carried on giving directions "A little bit further Alan and you'll see the big oak", Alan was by now in one hell of a mood, he was a mostly calm person but had been known in the past to lose his cool in certain situations, he could feel that his expensive clothes where thick with mud, his feet felt heavy due to the clumps of earth stuck to them and he was cold and frightened, all the ingredients needed for Alan to lose his temper.

The large bright moon which hung in the sky shone down a tiny piece of light through the trees to a clearing where a great old oak tree proudly stood “I can see the tree” Alan explained “and you never answered my question” he stated.

Again, in Alans opinion, he felt there was a sense that the kidnapper was ignoring Alan’s question, instead of answering it, the voice on the phone carried on with the instructions “this is the easy part Alan, all you do is lay the bag by the tree and then walk back to where you came from” said the voice, Alan walked the few yards left and reached the tree, he dropped the bag and leant against the trees old trunk and took a minute, with the phone to his ear he tried one last time to get some information out of the kidnapper, “why do you avoid the question”? Alan asked in an abrupt kind of way, this time the reply came instantly and harshly “I’m not here to be questioned, I’m here to tell what you need to do, so stop with the bullshit and drop the fucking bag” said the voice.

Alan was shocked at the hostility and stood for a few seconds in silence just trying to take it all in. He moved the bag with his foot, so it was touching the tree then spoke into the phone again "the bag is next to the tree" he said, the kidnapper slowly adjusted the lens on the night vision goggles and zoomed in to see the bag laid on the ground just like Alan said, "so what now"? Said Alan, the kidnapper replied, "you go back to the car park and await instructions" he said.

Alan felt his heart suddenly speed up, the blood was pumping faster through his veins, his eyes had become wider, he was feeling anger, and true rage now seemed to be controlling him "fuck you arse hole, I'm not waiting for anymore instructions, my job was to drop off the bag and I've done it, so you tell me now and don't ignore me, where is my sister" He shouted down the phone, several seconds ticked by without a word being spoken by either man, Alan never moved, he remained with his back leant against the tree and waited to hear the kidnappers voice, then Alan became tired of waiting, he was half a second from launching a loud and cutting verbal attack on the kidnapper, the voice on the phone however stopped him in his tracks when a calm and controlled reply came through.

“My dad used to always tell me and my brother, that there is nothing wrong if a person has a temper, it only becomes a problem when that person loses it” said the voice, in a preaching way “A bit like you just lost your temper then” the voice carried on, there was a small pause while the kidnapper

checked on his surroundings before making a move closer to the oak tree “don’t forget the situation you’re in and try to hold onto that temper of yours Alan” Alan knew the kidnapper was right, he took a breath to calm himself down “I’m sorry, you must appreciate the stress I’m under right now” Alan said apologetically “all I want is my sister back, you have your money so will you please tell me where she is" Alan pleaded with the kidnapper.

"When you get back to your car, look for a dark blue Volvo estate, its parked in the shadows and hard to find but it's there" explained the voice "when you find it, your sister is asleep in the back of it, she's not been harmed in any way, and the effects of the tranquilisers will wear off after an hour or two" the voice carried on saying.

this reply sounded like sweet music to Alan, he ran off as fast as he could, considering the terrain, retracing his steps back along the sloppy mud path and through the forest, as he did on the trek up to the tree, he tripped and fell over several times as he raced back down to the car park.

The thought of his younger sister being frightened and in the hands of the kidnapper made him feel sick and emotional, It was natural instinct, courage and tenacity which carried him along.

At times when Alan fell or slipped he hurt himself, on one occasion when he fell he cracked the back of his head on what Alan thought was a tree stump, and then on another occasion he fell face first into some stinging nettles, making his face feel like it was tingling but not in a pleasant way, this was more like his face was burning.

Alan knew that once all this was over and he began to get himself cleaned up, that he would discover cuts, grazes, bruises and lumps all over his body, acting as evidence of his many falls.

With the help of the adrenaline, which was pumping through his body, he could handle the pain, however he knew that when tonight was over that the pain would torture him when the adrenaline had worn off.

The voice on the phone began to speak to Alan, “slow down Alan, or you’ll end up breaking a leg or something” he said in an excitable tone. Alan was not listening and was ignoring the voice, and instead he was using the light from the phone, to find his way back to a deserted car park.

The kidnapper, stayed at the top where he could see the tree and the bag of money, and he watched Alan for as long as he could before he disappeared out of sight, the journey back had seemed to be over in half the time it took Alan to get there.

Whilst Alan was busy finding his way back to the car park and now out of sight of the kidnapper, he decided that it was now safe to approach the oak tree, he opened the bag and checked its contents, he allowed himself a smile as he saw the stacks of cash stuffed inside.

He zipped up the bag, flung it over his shoulder and quickly and gracefully ran through the dark forest, the night vision goggles helping him guide his way, he ran in-between the trees and across streams in the opposite direction to where Alan was heading. With the bag securely on his back, he ran the few miles like a royal marine in training.

Alan had reached the car park and was completely caked in mud, from his shoes to his hair, he hurriedly jumped into his car not caring for the leather upholstery, reversed out of the space he occupied and with lights on full beam he began to drive around the car park.

Although he drove slowly, every fibre of his being was yelling at him to speed up, to go faster but common sense prevailed, he couldn't afford to miss the Volvo and this place was so dark he could be parked right next to it and still not see it, especially with the hanging fog getting thicker. So, he drove at a snail's pace. Staying in first gear he approached the bend of the car park when his lights caught the shape of a dark car about ten meters to his left, the vehicle was obscured, it had been parked in-between a set of bushes so remaining hidden, even though he wasn't sure if it was the Volvo he quickly jumped out of his car to make sure, as he approached the car he recognised the box shape of a Volvo and tried the back doors which were locked, he looked closely through the window but saw nothing but blackness, Alan walked

around to the back of the car muttering to himself "this must be the car, it has to be" as he spoke he pulled the lever on the rear tailgate of the car which wasn't locked, he lifted it open and as he did the car's interior light came on to reveal a person who Alan immediately recognised as his sister, she was motionless, but looked at first glance to be unharmed and peaceful as she lay in a drug induced sleep.

The rear seats had been lifted forward and she was laid face up on the clean carpet of the back of the car, she had been wrapped in warm blankets so to fend off the cold and her head was comfortably resting on a pillow, Alan crawled into the back and checked her over, she was doped up and asleep but she was alive and had a strong pulse, Reaching into his pocket he immediately used his phone and informed Jo Tucker that Lauren was safe. Alan knelt next to her with her head resting on his lap as he stroked her hair and waited for help to arrive.

As Alan sat waiting, in less than minute after he had made the phone call he heard a helicopter scream by overhead, Alan looked through the cars windows and could see the lights of the helicopter disappear into the night as it travelled in search of the kidnapper.

In the distance he could hear the sounds of sirens and dogs barking, the helicopter was now circling small areas of the forest with its search beam scouring the area, DI Tucker and her trusted sergeant pulled up in a car, and both approached the Volvo, Tucker showed genuine concern when speaking to Alan "how is she"? She enquired, Alan laid his sisters head gently back onto the pillow and crawled out of the back of the car, "she's been drugged, but she seems ok, any chance of an ambulance getting here"? Alan said as he attempted to wipe away some of the mud from his clothing.

Tucker gave Alan a gentle smile "there is one on the way, it won't be long" she replied, Alan turned and looked at his sleeping sister, as he did Tucker put her right hand onto his shoulder "you did well Alan, because of you your sister is alive, and the net is closing in on this guy".

Tucker saw Alan wipe away a tear of relief from his cheek, he felt overwhelmed as the stress and the worry that had hung above him for over a week was suddenly all lifted from him, leaving him feeling numb inside, Tucker reached into her pocket and handed Alan a small packet of tissues “it’s the emotion of it all” she said, Alan took the tissues and smiled

at Tucker, he wiped his eyes and blew his nose “you’ll get this bastard won’t you”? he asked, Tucker gave him a big beaming smile “he’s already on borrowed time, if he manages to give us the slip tonight, we have a tracking device fitted to some of the notes which is going to lead me straight to him”, Alan looked at Tucker with astonishment, “I’m too clever for them Alan, too clever for them all, no one gets away from me” she said proudly.

CHAPTER FIVE

The cellar was in silence, the three captives were watching Reid as he pulled up a chair and sat facing them. He placed his mobile on the work bench next to the vice and placed his pistol next to the phone; he stretched out his arms high above his head and gave out a huge yawn, "I haven't slept in such a long time" he said, making an exaggerated yawning sound. Reid looked at Pengilly and Chambers "although I don't suppose you two have slept much either" he then looked at Russell "however, you spent last night in your comfy bed, so these two will be pretty envious of you" he said referring to Chambers and Pengilly.

Reid got to his feet and approached the three, with his right hand he took hold of one corner of the tape which covered the mouth of Pengilly and quickly pulled it off, it was done quickly enough to alleviate most of the pain but left the skin around his mouth reddened, Pengilly reacted with the discomfort but refrained from speaking out through fear and avoided eye contact with Reid.

Reid went down the line and pulled the tape from the mouths of all three men; he rolled the tape into a ball and threw it at the head of Chambers, who muttered under his breath as it bounced of his forehead "what was that"? Asked Reid, Chambers didn't answer, he put his head down and stared at his hands which where tightly fastened to the table, Russell immediately looked at Pengilly "what are you doing here" he enquired, "I know as much as you do" Pengilly replied with a whisper.

Reid smirked, now he had complete control of the situation he felt more relaxed and now he wasn't against the clock he didn't have to think quickly, and it meant less things could go wrong.

Reid began to walk amongst the wine racks as he spoke, taking a good look at some of the expensive bottles in Russell's collection.

"No one has to die today, but saying that, if someone tries anything stupid, then that someone will be shot" he explained in a confident tone, Reid chose a bottle of red at random, he wiped away the dust to reveal the label which was written in a foreign language and looked very old, it was faded in parts as if it had been stood in direct sun light and some of the writing had been worn away.

Reid studied it for a few seconds then attempted to read it out loud but gave up half way through, he approached Russell and showed him the bottle "how do you say that"? He asked, Russell took one quick glance and read it out in a French accent "Chateau Margaux Balthazar", Reid looked at the bottle then back at Russell “how much is it worth”? He asked, “Approximately four thousand pounds” replied Russell with disdain.

Reid, sensing the tone in Russell’s voice, let the bottle slip from his fingers, the four men witnessed as it fell to the floor, for Russell it fell in slow motion, he watched in horror as the bottle made contact with the cold and dry concrete floor, the bottle shattered into a dozen pieces, the red wine inside splashed out staining the pale grey concrete a deep red colour, the wine splashed up onto some of the walls, with some landing on Reid’s trousers and shoes. Russell closed his eyes and turned away not wanting to see part of his collection destroyed.

“Oops, sorry about that” said Reid sarcastically as he kicked the fragments of glass toward the wall, “you’re not sorry at all” replied Russell. Reid never replied but simply walked amongst the racks again, this time he chose to leave the wine bottles where they were on the racks, and instead he just walked up and down the aisle making a rough estimate of how many bottles where in Russell's collection.

After a few minutes had passed he reappeared from the wine racks and walked back to the table and faced the three "you must have over two hundred and fifty bottles here Oliver" said Reid directing his conversation to Russell, Russell thought for a second, pondering on whether to answer or not, he had to be smart, he had no idea what Reid was capable of, but he had just taken three men hostage and was armed with a gun, so decided that the best thing to do would be to engage Reid in conversation "I think it's more like three hundred, is that what this is about, a wine robbery?, because I can save you some time, you will have plenty of problems trying to sell these on unless you're stealing it to order in which case you won't get even a quarter of their actual price" replied Russell, hoping to educate Reid on what he thought was a badly planned robbery.

Reid sat down again opposite the three men; he looked calm and relaxed as he leant back in the chair "this isn't a wine robbery, it isn't a robbery full stop, and I wouldn't need these two if I was just here to rob you of your wine" said Reid referring to Chambers and Pengilly.

Reid, who had a curious look on his face, carried on talking "just out of interest though, how much are all those bottles worth"? He asked, Russell maintained eye contact with Reid, suddenly feeling a little more confident before he answered "my best estimate would be" Russell paused for a short while as he calculated the figure in his head "five hundred thousand pounds, maybe more" he stated proudly considering the situation he was in.

There was an intense silence between the men, Reid moved his eyes along the line, staring at each man for a while with an expressionless face, the three men looked back at him then looked at each other nervously before the silence was broken by Pengilly "for the love of god, are you going to explain what all this is about"? He said with a raised voice, the other two looked at Pengilly in shock that he could find the courage to speak out.

Reid got to his feet and stood at the table directly in front of the three, he spoke confidently and with some authority as if he had practiced the speech a thousand times "Of course you three know each other, but I'm surprised that not one of you have figured out who I am" he pointed to Pengilly and Russell who both looked puzzled, Reid carried on "for so called intelligent men, its taking some working out isn't it? let me explain" Reid picked up his chair and moved it to where he had been standing and sat down, again facing the three men, he pointed at Pengilly first and began to reveal the big mystery "you're Brian Pengilly, a high court judge, and a member of the British empire, congratulations on that by the way, I spent two decades risking my life for her majesty and she never gave me an MBE" this statement left Pengilly speechless.

He then moved his attention over to Russell "and you are Oliver Bilton Russell, a barrister in criminal law and by all accounts a very good one, expensive, but very good" both men listened in silence.

Reid then stood and faced Chambers, his demeanour changed in an instant, it was as if a black cloud had descended over him and his face gave the contorted image of a dangerous animal who is moments away from striking, through gritted teeth he spoke “And you are Craig Chambers, you come from a long line of thieves and petty criminals, you are a heroin addict and a dirty lying bastard and you were meant to be waking up in prison this morning, having been sentenced to five years for death by dangerous driving, after you stole an innocent woman’s car and then ran her down in it, killing her instantly” just like Pengilly and Russell, Chambers sat in silence and just looked at Reid, the fear etched all over his face.

With Reid staring deep into the eyes of Chambers, there was nothing said for some time before the silence was broken once again by Pengilly “so you know who we are, who are you”? he questioned, Reid explained “the woman killed that night was, as you all know, called Rebecca Reid, my name is Steven Reid, I am, correction, I was her Husband”.

As soon as the sentence left Reid's mouth it was met with a mixture of shock and astonishment, Russell and Chambers immediately looked at each other, Chambers quickly broke the gaze and looked down at his hands again, he began to feel sick with fear.

Reid, who was purposely introducing the dramatic silences to his speech, so as to let the information sink in and to give the mind time to think therefore building the tension and fear to what could be described as palpable, was again standing in silence after making the announcement and yet again it was left to Pengilly to break the it "Ok, so now we have an idea of your motive for doing what you're doing, but what is it exactly that you have planned?" this time Russell, who had found some confidence spoke as well "Baring in mind Mr Reid that the police are no doubt outside as we speak and considering you took me at gunpoint there will be snipers outside all of which have the full intention of getting you in their crosshairs" Russell spat the last line of the sentence out in a hurry due to fear and a shortage of breath. Reid smiled smugly and replied to the statement “I’ll answer your question first of all judge, what I have planned is simple, I plan to get to the truth of what happened that night” Russell interrupted “the truth came out in court, and it was very straight forward, Young chambers stole an expensive car, as he sped away he didn’t see the woman, who we now know is your wife, she stepped out into the road and he ran her down, unfortunately she died and chambers has been punished”.

Reid replied to Russell with a similar disdain he had received “that was the version that came out in court, but that was a bit to orchestrated for my liking, a bit too simple, a bit too” he paused for a brief moment his eyes looked upwards as if thinking of the word he wanted to use “bullshitty” he said, “I want things done this time without the rules that give courts of law its limitations” Reid added, all this time chambers sat with his head bowed not saying a word, Russell replied to Reid’s allegations “it was determined in a court of law, you don’t get any higher than that for Christ's sake, all the evidence was studied and all the witnesses who saw it gave their evidence under oath" Reid had his views on the court case, but he wasn't prepared to go into it at that time, he had plenty of time for that.

Of course, Russell and Pengilly would be on the side of the justice system, since they worked in that profession, and Reid knew that, but Reid had a few points to prove and he would be proving them when the time was right.

Reid made no comment to Russell's reply, instead he changed the subject "As for the police and their crack marksmen being outside, I hope they are, that's the whole idea, I'm relying

on them being there" he said as he began to walk around the cellar again, every now and then he would glance over at

Chambers who sat with his head down and in silence, his skinny frame hunched over, and showing obvious signs of fear.

Reid's confidence was rising, in his head he imagined himself snapping the neck of Chambers, he wanted nothing more than to do that, but then he would remind himself that would be a quick death, and Chambers should be made to suffer, like he was suffering.

Reid took a glance upwards towards the ceiling and noted that they were rafters that he could easily throw a rope over and tie the other end to Chambers' neck, then slowly pull on the rope lifting chambers up into the air and watch him kick and struggle as the air is slowly squeezed from his body.

Reid had seen and done this in the past and he pictured Chambers' last few twitches as his body gives up through lack of oxygen, his brain eventually dies, and his heart gives out one last, very weak beat until he finally passes away after several minutes of agony.

That is the way Chambers should die, Reid thought, and he wanted so much to just do it right at that moment, but he managed to remain in control, he managed to stick to the plan, the plan he had put together in a short space of time during the trial and he had been so methodical with, he knew that this plan would work and he had to follow his strict guide lines.

As he walked slowly and aimlessly around the cellar he began to inform the three men of how things would play out. "Before your wife ran out into the street Oliver, I handed her a piece of paper which had my mobile number on it" again Reid was drawn to some of the bottles of wine on the racks and with great care this time, he picked up the odd one.

Russell looked on in despair as he expected another bottle to be dropped to the floor, but Reid simply inspected it and replaced it slowly and carefully back on the rack from where he had got it, whilst doing this he carried on talking.

"I'm expecting whoever is in charge out there to ring me at some stage then we can get on with what we need to do while we

are down here" Reid wandered back over to where the three men where sat and continued "until then, not a lot is going to be happening so we might as well make some small talk" Reid looked at the three for inspiration on a subject they could discuss but was met with silence, he sat down slowly and with a sigh he finished off by saying “or if you prefer, we could just sit in silence”.

Again no one spoke, after a brief moment Reid shot to his feet quickly, which startled Chambers “but I prefer small talk” Reid pointed out, “I have a question for you Oliver” he said quickly and confidently.

Russell, mainly to humour Reid, obliged by asking what the question was. Reid went ahead and asked, “how do you sleep at night knowing that because of your skills in law that some real dangerous and nasty criminals are walking the streets” Reid said with a look of intrigue, looking forward to the answer about to come his way.

Russell had heard this kind of question several times before, he knew that every defence barrister had, it wasn't the first

time a disapproving member of public or a disgruntled relative of a victim had slung that kind of remark at him and it probably wouldn't be the last, so he answered it in the same way he always did. "Everyone is entitled to a defence; British law believes in fairness thankfully" was the somewhat rehearsed reply.

What surprised Russell however was Reid's response "I couldn't agree more" said Reid, who then went for another wander amongst the wine racks, this left Russell at a loss for words, in the past he has had to defend his job and his whole career to people who had come at him with the same argument but on this occasion and considering the circumstances he wasn't expecting the response he received from Reid.

Reid, however wasn't finished, he was simply putting Russell off balance, as he walked amongst the racks, purposely looking nonchalant he carried on with his line of questioning "that's not what I asked though" Reid said in a raised voice as he was now over the other side of the cellar, obscured by the racks and out of sight from the others.

Russell looked over trying to see Reid "what exactly is your question?" he asked, Reid peered from around the racks, only his head and shoulders visible "I asked how you sleep at night? when because of you there are murderers, rapists and generally dangerous people walking the streets" Russell let out a disappointed sigh "here we go, have you any idea how many times I've heard that question?" Russell replied, Reid reappeared from amongst the racks and approached the bench "then you shouldn't have any trouble answering it" he said.

Russell shook his head "I have answered it, I said that everyone is entitled to a defence, and I offer them that" he replied with agitation in his voice, Reid, sensing Russell's agitation, began to put more pressure "so you said, but I want to know how you feel about that, do you feel comfortable knowing that some scroats commit crimes that can destroy people's lives? And it's because of you that they were out on the streets to be able to commit those crimes in the first place" Reid said becoming animated with his actions.

Maybe it was because of the situation that Russel was in, he never usually got agitated whenever he was asked this question, but he could feel himself becoming more uptight, and for that brief moment he didn't care that Reid was a dangerous man with a gun "I sleep fine thank you, better than you do probably" he said with so much contempt that Pengilly threw him a look to warn him to be careful.

That remark, or one just like it, was what Reid had been hoping for, he suddenly became more serious, standing in front of Russell, he focussed on him and him alone, he could see the other two in his peripheral vision but his attention was all on Russell "you're right, you probably do sleep better than me, but I've seen and been a part of some very horrible things" Reid replied, his eyes fixed on Russell with Russell staring right back at him.

Reid could feel the tension between the two building "I've been in war zones and seen kids as young as seventeen lose limbs or be killed, some hardened soldiers have even lost their minds because of what they witnessed or had to endure" Reid carried on, now with the full attention of all three men, who were listening intently.

Reid never broke his stare from Russell as he spoke "I myself have been dropped over enemy lines, and had to fight for my life, outnumbered and petrified, with only my training to fall back on, it was kill or be killed, so I killed and I've killed a lot of people, in fact if the queen knew exactly how many people I've killed in her name, then she wouldn't sleep to well at night either" At this point Reid's attention was grabbed by Pengilly who interjected with his opinion "that is all very sad and I have to say, very admirable of you to fight for the freedom of others, but you signed up to join the forces, no one forced you, so you can't use that as an excuse if you're suffering from post-traumatic stress, or feeling guilt" said Pengilly.

Reid broke his stare from Russell and glanced over at the judge "I'm suffering from neither judge, certainly not guilt, all I wanted to know, before we all became interested in my sleeping pattern, is Russell comfortable fighting for the freedom of the guilty" Reid replied, then switched his gaze back over to Russell, who paused for a few seconds before answering "Yes I am comfortable with it, because if I get someone off you can bet that they are either innocent or the investigation is flawed in some way, meaning a prosecution would be unsafe" Russell replied, Reid thought about Russell's honest answer for a moment "plus you earn a shit load of cash" he replied.

Russell certainly wasn't embarrassed by how much he earned, his ego meant that he was very proud of the fact he was wealthy and he showed his wealth as often and in any way he could, and with a broad smile he answered Reid "yes, I earn a shit load of cash, as you poetically put it" there was one subject that Russell felt more comfortable discussing than any other and that was his wealth, and it seemed that they were now on that topic.

Reid felt Russell's enjoyment, so decided it would be short lived "that's exactly what's wrong with the world" he said in a lecturer's tone "a footballer can earn a hundred grand a week, an actor can earn millions for one film, you probably earn several hundreds of thousand every year just for talking on some scum bags behalf in court, but I and many like me risk our lives many times to protect this country and we don't earn even a small percentage of that kind of money" Reid pointed out.

This never bothered Russell and his smile remained but Reid had one more question for him "answer me this Oliver, if it was your mother or father who had been robbed at gun point by a prolific violent armed robber, or your son who had been given drugs that killed him by a drug dealer with a long record or your daughter who had been raped by a serial rapist, what would you think about the person who was defending them?" Reid stood and waited eagerly for the reply, the smile on Russell's face disappeared as quickly as it appeared "ill refer you to my original answer, everyone is entitled to a defence" he said very flippantly.

Reid remained quiet for a while to let the answer go in "and that has answered my question on how you sleep at night, that's how you manage to sleep at all, by telling yourself that, even though people like you make the streets even more dangerous than they already are, you keep telling yourself that, so you can sleep soundly in your king size" was Reid's reply.

Reid turned and sat himself down on the chair, he placed himself into a leant back and relaxed position and the cellar then fell quiet, leaving Russell to think about the

discussion, while Reid just listened to the silence while there was some.

CHAPTER SIX

The scene outside the house was one of chaos, the once quiet and affluent area had been taken over by dozens of police cars and officers, who had closed off both entrances to the road leading to the house and police officers on foot were busy evacuating all the nearby occupants of the other houses.

The air was filled with the sounds of barking police dogs, police radio chatter and the sirens of arriving emergency service vehicles. A helicopter hovered above the house checking the scale and layout of the building and relaying any relevant information to the people on the ground.

Deep underground in the cellar, Reid's silent moment was broken when he and the three prisoners began to slightly hear the action going on outside. The sound of sirens brought a sly smile of relief to Russell's face and he glanced over at the judge for reassurance that things were going to be ok, however the sly smile was wiped from the face of Russell when he noticed that the judge's expression remained just as cold and just as stony, it suddenly became apparent to Russell that the judge did not share his sense of hope that this will all soon be over, and it was with that single glance over at the judge when he slowly realised that it was far from over and that it was only the beginning, there was a long way to go.

Outside the house and directly in the entrance of the long and wide driveway the police had blocked any entrance through the neatly varnished solid wooden gates. They had parked a long wheel base white van directly over the entrance to the gates, along the side of the van where written the words, 'Mobile Incident Command Unit'.

It was the brand-new investment made by the police force as the command unit included all the latest cutting edge technology including CCTV cameras, recording equipment, sound enhancing devices and any item needed which would aid the police in investigating any crime committed that required a unit at the scene.

It had cost the force hundreds of thousands of pounds and meant that the police could set to work immediately and remain at the scene for the entire duration of the incident, and at an incident such as this one it was ideal.

With everything set up the police where now hanging around for direction from a senior officer who was yet to arrive, as some officers monitored the CCTV footage of the front of the house from inside the van, others outside where huddled in several groups killing time until they were given a task to do.

After a short while an official looking car arrived and parked up just on the outskirts of the cordon, from the passenger seat stepped Jo Tucker, instantly visible was the annoyed look on her face, she flashed her badge at the officer guarding the cordon and he cordially lifted the tape for Tucker to enter.

She determinedly walked the sixty or so meters toward the command unit, neither looking at nor communicating with any other person she passed on her way. She climbed the two steps up to the door and swung it open, as she marched in she noticed the half dozen officers inside, who had all turned to face her as she burst into the unit.

Tucker stood for a few seconds, just taking in her surroundings then gave her first address "for those who don't know me, ask someone who does, all you really need to know right at this moment is that I'm now in charge of this entire operation and I'm pretty pissed off about it".

Tucker had been investigating the kidnapping of Lauren Harley for the past week and had tracked her kidnapper through a large forest in the early hours of the morning, unfortunately and to Tuckers dissatisfaction the kidnapper managed to slip through the very tight net that Tucker had set for him, mainly because of his knowledge of the area and his planning of the operation.

However, Tucker always had a backup plan and the tracking device which had been inserted into the bundles of ransom money had lead armed police to an ordinary terraced house, and as daylight broke they had burst in and apprehended a man, who said very little upon arrest but showed definite signs of bewilderment as to what had lead the police to his door.

The scene was set then for Tucker, after only a few hours' rest, to get the man into an interview room and then charged with kidnap.

Tucker loved the game, as she often put it, she loved everything that went into a case, as she saw it, it was her versus an opponent, her brains and skills against those of whoever she was up against.

But it was the interview she loved the most, during the investigation stage, when she is engaged in tracking down and chasing the suspect, she usually has no idea who it is that her and her team are looking for and that sense of mystery gave her the enjoyment, but once the suspect has been caught and jo has them in the interview room she really goes to work.

She is, at that stage, face to face with that person, she can look into their eyes, she can read their reactions she can pre-empt their lies and counter act their stories or defence with perfectly gathered evidence, and Tucker got a real kick out of beating someone in the interview and she got even a bigger kick when the suspects solicitor gets involved only for Jo to beat them as well.

She always says to her officers or anyone wishing to learn from her that failing to plan is planning to fail and she

never went into an interview without having a plan and all the evidence she needed to back it up.

It was set to be a very easy case, the kidnapper was very confident that the police would never be able to track him through the woods, and he was right, as they didn't, but his confidence became his down fall as he made no effort to manage the evidence that he had accumulated during the kidnap and ransom drop.

He hadn't yet got around to clearing the garage he rented which was situated just fifty meters from his house, inside was the ropes he had used to tie his victim up with and also a map of the forest which he had chosen for the money to be handed over and if that wasn't enough his boots and the clothes he wore during the drop were sat in a bin bag waiting to be destroyed, they were covered in the mud from the forest which could easily be analysed and proven that the mud was indeed from that area of the forest.

Instead he had celebrated with half a bottle of whisky and gone to bed secure in the knowledge that he was safe, Jo thought to herself upon the arrest and search of the man's house and garage, that after all the careful planning and the very clever way of collecting the ransom money, this man had let himself down badly by being sloppy and not getting rid of all the evidence, he had simply become too complacent and had let his confidence rule his head which had now sealed his fate and Jo, who had never lost the feeling of excitement and exhilaration that she felt when making a big arrest and securing a prosecution, was preparing herself for yet another case that she had successfully closed.

However, it never worked out that way as she was ordered by her senior officer to attend the siege, solely on the basis that she was a trained negotiator and was the only one available at that time, she was annoyed at the fact that all her hard work had now been handed over to someone else to finish off, there was one thing that used to grind Tuckers gears and it was not seeing a job through from beginning to end.

She knew it was pointless arguing or debating the matter, so she sucked it up and briefed her replacement on what he needed to know about the kidnap case and then made her way to the siege.

At the end of the day, and as was pointed out to her by her superintendent, a successful prosecution was a positive result for the police force as a whole and for the public and it was not about a single officer scoring points or taking credit.

Tucker though did see it that way, although she never let it be known, she played the game to win and she always won, and she hated that the victory had been taken away from her at her favourite part.

CHAPTER SEVEN

Tucker had her work to do but as she did that Reid was sat in silence along with the three hostages, inside the cold cellar, with his head slightly lowered and staring at the floor without blinking he was sat motionless as if in a trance like state, the other three quietly sat and watched him.

The thing going through Reid's mind at that moment and which was taking up all his attention was flash backs of the court case, that subject would often have Reid going over and over the proceedings for hours at a time in his head.

He remembered feeling like the loneliest man in the world as he sat in the corridors of the court waiting to be allowed into the gallery, Rebecca had no family, both her parents, who were without siblings, had passed away some years earlier and she was an only child herself.

Reid also never had any family, he grew up in care homes all his young life and had then joined the army the minute he turned sixteen, of course he had some great and loyal army buddies but right then and there he was all alone and was about to find out how and hopefully why his wife of nine years was killed.

Reid sat silent throughout the entire court case, for three long weeks he was first to arrive and last to leave the court house; his only contact was the police officer leading the investigation into his wife's death.

He sat and watched as witness after witness gave their evidence of what happened, and Reid took it all in, he had a very sharp mind and could tell when something wasn't right and it was during the questioning of the defendant Chambers that Reid knew something definitely was not right.

Chambers' barrister that day, as he stood in the dock wearing an ill-fitting suit, was Bilton Russell, the same man who he was tied up next to and being held against his will with. On that day in court Reid watched as Russell cleverly lead his client along with some well worked out question and answer sessions.

Craig Chambers was so averse to wearing a suit that on the odd occasion when he needed to, for court appearances mainly, he seemed to make other people who were witness to this strange phenomenon, nervous and uneasy at what they were seeing, he was so thin that it was difficult to find clothes that fitted him properly, so he usually wore tracksuits and T shirts which always hung off him but they looked less odd, a suit however did look odd as it draped off his bony physique with his long thin neck along with his pale sucked in face stuck out the top of the collar of the shirt, reminiscent of a tortoise without a shell.

As he stood in the witness box, swearing to almighty god to tell the truth the whole truth and nothing but, wearing the cheap grey suit which, judging by the creases all over it, had spent its time since it was last worn rolled up in the bottom of a wardrobe, even the collar on his pale blue shirt had unsightly creases on it, and the Windsor knot in his tie simply told Reid that someone else had tied it for him.

He spoke very slowly and clearly when giving evidence, a slight nervous tremor could be detected in his voice, but it was plain for Reid to see that his answers had been rehearsed,

Bilton Russell started off his line of questioning by getting Chambers to explain his movements that day "can you explain to the court what you were doing on the day in question" asked Russell.

Chambers took a deep breath before he spoke "I had taken some heroin on the morning" answered Chambers before Russell informed the jury of some important information with a planned interruption, "may I inform the court that Mr Chambers did have a drug problem at the time of the incident but has since voluntarily entered himself onto a drugs rehabilitation and detox programme" explained Russell very proudly before instructing Chambers to continue with his evidence.

“Later that afternoon I had taken quite a few lines of coke and had been smoking marijuana most of the day also” Chambers told the court, Russell then expertly drained every bit of relevant and important information out of Chambers.

He explained that he was feeling very high after taking the cocktail of drugs and had taken himself off for a walk, Chambers pointed out that he had nowhere in particular to go

and was just walking, he mentioned that the weather, which had started off mild for early December, had taken a sudden drop in temperature, it was pointed out to the court that Chambers was only wearing jeans T shirt and tracksuit top and that as the effects of the drugs began to wear off he began to feel the cold which he described as cutting through him right to the bone. He claims that before he knew it he had been walking around for hours and suddenly realized that he had no idea where he was.

Chambers explained that he never noticed until that moment that he was no longer in the outskirts of town and was now in an area which was surrounded by the countryside, the quaint high street of the quiet village he found himself in had people wandering around, most of which were looking at Chambers with concern, not only was he a stranger in town but he was one who looked like trouble, straight away these simple country folk had spotted the stereotypical drug addict and where beginning to feel nervous at his presence.

Chambers went on to say that he began to panic at being lost and convinced himself that he needed a car for him to be able to get home, he says that he walked from the high street and

headed further out of the village when he ended up on a quiet country road with a row of a dozen secluded cottages which stood alone opposite a wooded area, it was here that he spotted the silver land rover parked half on the kerb directly outside one of the cottages and because it was over ten years old he knew that it would be fairly easy to steal.

Chambers then went on to explain to the jury exactly how he stole the car. "After snapping off the plastic ignition housing it was just the matter of joining up the wires which starts the engine" he explained. He mentioned that he chose the car because of its age and that the area was very dark and quiet, so there was little chance of him being disturbed.

Russell, with some intelligent questioning, lead Chambers to explain how he felt the blast of warm air coming from the heater vents as the engine roared into life and how it felt on his freezing skin. "Because I was so cold, parts of my body felt numb" explained Chambers in a quiet controlled voice, "When the warm air hit me, it felt great, and I sat for a moment just enjoying the warmth, then I remembered that I never had the time and I'd still feel the warmth as I drove along, I knew I had a car to steal so I went to work" Chambers

told the court, with Russell giving him a reassuring smile as he gave his evidence.

The engine was very loud he recalled, and he was concerned that some of the neighbours might hear it. As soon as the engine started he quickly closed the door and switched off any interior lights so as to not attract any unwanted attention, he then slipped it into first gear and began to drive away.

It wasn't long, recalled Chambers, before he had manoeuvred off the kerb and had picked up his speed and was just about to move from second gear into third when he felt the vehicle go over a bump, it felt as if he had driven over a speed bump a bit too fast, but then he remembers hearing a woman screaming.

Chambers went on to describe, whilst in a sombre and tearful mood, his account of what happened "after feeling the bump" he explained "I heard a scream and saw a woman running over to the car and shouting at me to stop, she told me I'd hit someone" he went on to explain that he immediately stopped the car and got out to look under the vehicle, it was then that he saw the body of a woman bent in half and stuck under the car and she wasn't moving, it was an image he explained that has haunted him ever since and will carry on doing so for the rest of his life.

He remembers feeling numb except on this occasion it was nothing to do with the cold, in fact because of the shock he said he suddenly couldn't feel the freezing cold anymore and he simply sat on the kerb waiting for the emergency services to arrive with his head in his hands, he explained to the jury that he couldn't stop himself from crying because of what had happened but insists that he did not see the woman when she stepped out in front of the car.

The prosecution where keen to point out that the land rover Chambers was stealing belonged to the dead woman and she was merely trying to stop the theft of the vehicle by running out in front of it, it was at this point she was struck by the big heavy car which was travelling more than twenty miles an hour and when she was hit by the car her body was dragged underneath snapping her spine.

The prosecution barrister was going for the angle that the dead woman would still be alive today if Chambers had not decided to steal the car, However, in his defence statement Russell had pointed out that his client had admitted that he stole the car but he was on trial to decide if he was telling the truth about him simply not seeing the woman as he drove away, Russell had made it clear to the jury that Chambers had sworn under oath that it was an accident and because it was dark and she was wearing dark clothing that he didn't see her.

Being the top professional he was he also made the point that Chambers has indeed got a long criminal record, most of which was done through his dependence on drugs but his crimes where for petty offences and he would not ever intentionally physically hurt another person.

Russell had the jury eating out of the palm of his hand at one point as he went through in detail just how difficult it had been for Chambers, with the nightmares of that night regularly waking him up and the immense feeling of guilt that he cannot deal with and since sought professional help in the form of a counsellor.

He pointed out that his client had attempted suicide because of the guilt of taking an innocent woman's life. And how he was now on antidepressants, "Mr Chambers has now made huge steps at changing his life, he no longer takes drugs and he genuinely wants to stop living a life of crime and wants to do things differently and for the better" Russell pointed out "He now wants to be sent to prison as he wants to be punished" Russell went on to say "but I believe it would only be fair to hand my client a custodial sentence for the crime he has committed, which is vehicle theft and driving while under the influence of drugs and not for anything else because I think, as we've proved, he did not intend or mean to kill the lady at the scene and so he should not be punished for it, as my client is already being punished enough" Russell expertly explained to the court.

Chambers went on to explain that he will never forgive himself for the death of that lady. And as Reid watched on from the gallery he could feel the anger building in the pit of his stomach as he saw, what he thought would be a fair outcome, slipping away.

That woman was of course Rebecca Reid, the wife of Steven. She had been visiting a friend and was just leaving the house and was saying goodbye to her friend on the doorstep when they both heard her car engine start up.

Immediately, claims the friend, Rebecca realised it was her car that was being stolen so ran out onto the road to block its path when she was hit and fell to the floor, Medical examiners said during the trial that it wasn't at this point that Rebecca had died, it was when the car drove over her; it was at that point that her friend ran and banged on the window of the car causing it to stop.

Reid sat without any expression on his face during most of the trial and he remained the same as the jury returned to the courtroom to give the verdict. After hours of deliberation, during which time Reid had just sat in the court waiting area, quiet and motionless, he ran things through in his head, he played out in his mind all the evidence that he had heard, and still he felt that things where a bit to neat and a bit too simple, surely if he felt that way then the jury would feel it too.

When the jury returned and everyone in the court room had been seated and waited to hear the verdict, the tension was bubbling when the foreman of the jury was asked to stand, and the judge asked if the jury had come to a verdict to which the foreman replied "yes, we have your honour" Pengilly then carried on "for the offence of vehicle theft, do you find the defendant guilty or not guilty"? Reid, sitting in the public gallery and sitting in the same seat that he had occupied during the entire trial, stared straight ahead as the foreman replied guilty to vehicle theft, there was a slight reaction from some of the spectators in the public gallery, as Chambers was also found guilty of driving whilst under the influence of illegal substances, but it wasn't this offence that Reid was interested in, it was the next question that the judge was about to ask that Reid was waiting to hear.

Judge Pengilly cleared his throat and addressed the foreman once again. “For the offence of death by dangerous driving, do you find the defendant guilty or not guilty”? Reid held his breath for what seemed like a long time as he waited for the foreman to answer, he stared right at Chambers, his gaze burning into Chambers’ soul, Reid noticed that Chambers looked at ease, he showed little if no emotion at all as he waited for the verdict to be announced.

The foreman took a breath and replied, “not guilty” there were gasps of disbelief from the public gallery, some close friends and work colleagues of Rebecca shouted “no” as they were left stunned by the decision, Chambers celebrated with a smile and punched the air in delight, Reid as usual sat motionless and expressionless as his eyes drilled into Chambers who had no idea that he was being watched so intensely.

Judge Pengilly brought the court to order and then addressed the room; he instructed Chambers to stand and carried on "Craig Chambers, you have been found guilty for the offences of vehicle theft and driving whilst under the influence of drugs" There was a short pause by the judge as he allowed the now silent court room to take in what was being said before he continued.

"Your actions that day have caused a lot of grief and heartache and you have destroyed not just the life of Rebecca Reid but also her family and friends lives' have also been affected" as the judge spoke Reid listened intently to what was being said but he never took his eyes off Chambers for one second, "However it has been proven today that although your actions where wrong on the evening in question and you are

indeed, guilty of the two offences mentioned, you did not set out to hurt anyone as was pointed out to the court during your time in the witness box" as he spoke the entire court hung on his every word, "it is going to be very difficult for you to go through life now with the guilt of having accidently taken a life; I use the word accidently because that is what it was" Upon hearing the word accident Reid switched his stare from Chambers over to Pengilly for a brief moment before returning his gaze back to Chambers and continued listening to the judges summing up.

"A custodial sentence must be handed down to you today, but as the evidence suggests, the devastation that you caused that night because of your selfish and drug infused actions that this might have shocked you into changing your ways and turning your life around, I will advise you to throw yourself into your drugs rehab programme as that is the only way that you can take back control of your life" Pengilly's words echoed around the courtroom as he handed out a five-year sentence with the chance to apply for parole after eighteen months have been served.

After passing sentence Pengilly rose from his seat and exited the court room, he left some of the people in the public gallery with mixed emotions, with the fact that being found not guilty for death by dangerous driving was considered a win for them. It was Chambers' legal team who were celebrating with the result.

Reid seethed inside, he had several questions that he wanted answering, he didn't believe that chambers had walked over six miles from his house and ended up in the small leafy village by accident, why would he leave the house wearing just a tracksuit top when it was winter and why also did he not flee the scene?

For a career criminal like chambers it would be in his nature to run, to get away but he didn't that night.

It was questions like these and many more that was reason that Reid had decided to take the law in to his own hands and pull off the daring escape and hostage taking. However just like he believed chambers was being lead in the courtroom he needed a bit of leading himself and it came in an unlikely way.

CHAPTER EIGHT

The feeling of shock and disbelief wasn't pleasant for Reid, he ordered himself a coffee and moved along the line to the till and paid for it, it was freshly ground, piping hot and gave off that nice welcoming coffee smell and when it was received he found himself a quiet seat on his own at the back of the small coffee shop and while slowly sipping away at his beverage he ran through in his mind what had just happened in the court room.

Reid could only come up with the same answers over and over again and that was Chambers had killed his wife and had got away with it, he knew that it wasn't down to Chambers himself that he would be a free man in a couple of years, he was aware that Chambers wasn't smart enough, but he was even more aware that Bilton Russell was the person responsible, and that he had done an amazing job convincing the jury to believe their version of events.

As Reid sat deep in thought he became aware of a person standing at the table he was sitting at, the person then spoke "can I join you"? Said the voice, when Reid looked up he saw that it was Karen Caswell the detective sergeant who was heading up the team investigating Rebecca's death. Caswell was the first and last point of contact for Reid during the investigation and also during the trial.

She was early thirties and had been in the force since she was twenty years old, she had gone through several different mind sets during her career, in the beginning of her career she was in love with her job, she put in the hours and put in the hard work and she mixed this work ethic together with her ambition which saw her successfully promoted and also saw her gain plenty of experience and respect from most of her colleagues.

Over the years however she, like a lot of coppers, had her patience tested more times than she would like to remember, Just like everyone else she was over worked, under payed and quite often felt let down by her supervision, and this had turned her attitude from positive to negative and she found that she had been left with a bitter taste in her mouth after years and years of broken promises and what she believed was a total let down from the courts who seemed to have the criminals best interest at heart rather than those of the decent general public.

Caswell had nicked a heck of a lot of people and put a lot of people away for a long time, she knew of Craig Chambers but had never had any dealings with him and because within police circles he was one of the people that every police officer would like to send down for a very long time, Caswell felt the pressure of getting this right and not letting down her colleagues.

She was certain that she had everything covered going into the court case, she could see no way that Chambers wouldn't be sentenced for manslaughter, and that he would be starting a ten-year stretch, and that's another piece of scum off the streets for a long time.

Just like Reid, Caswell was stunned by the outcome, she also felt that she had let Reid down, she had kept him up to date during every step of the way during the trial and she had lead him to believe, mainly because she believed it herself, that Chambers would receive a punishment that matched the crime.

As she sat opposite Reid she was being very careful what she was saying, she sat with a take away cup of coffee in front of her and looked right at Reid "you must be feeling very let down right now" she said with compassion in her voice Reid didn't have to think of an answer "let down doesn't come close to how I'm feeling right now Karen" he replied staring at his reflection in the thick black coffee that sat in front of him.

Karen took a quick look around as if checking to see who was listening "sometimes it doesn't go our way, this is one of those times" Reid didn't reply and just sat with his head bowed still staring into his coffee.

"I think sometimes though that the law can never win in certain circumstances" continued Karen, she had lowered her tone and spoke slowly, and looking at the top of Reid's head she carried on "I'm just wondering how bad you want to get justice for what happened to Rebecca" Reid, on hearing her words slowly raised his head and looked directly at her, without a word being said Karen knew that Reid was interested so she carried on and spoke in hushed tones "I know for a fact that Chambers has another court appearance in a week's time, it's something to do with a different case, but he'll be travelling on a prison van on this day" Karen was interrupted by Reid "What are you suggesting Karen?" he asked, Karen took

another quick look around before answering "what do you think I'm suggesting Steven"? Reid sat in silence for a few seconds and shifted in his seat, trying to figure out in his head what it was that Karen meant, an overwhelming urge told him that what was going around in his mind, which was to take matters into his own hands and find out the truth in his own unique way, was exactly what Karen meant.

Karen handed Reid a folded piece of paper and stood up with her coffee to leave, she leant forward to speak to Reid before she left "If you're serious about getting justice, then meet me at this address tonight at nine, all your questions will be answered" Karen then turned and left the coffee shop with Reid watching her as she left, Reid opened up the piece of paper and looked at the address then folded it again and put it in his pocket and carried on drinking his coffee.

Reid was deep in thought as he finished his drink and left the coffee shop, this meeting with Karen was running through his mind as he walked to his car and it kept running through his mind as he drove home, He weighed up the pros and cons, on the one hand he knew the magnitude of what he wanted to do, and he knew that after breaking Chambers out of prison then holding him while he got the truth out of him in any way necessary, he would forfeit any liberty he once had as the police would hunt him down and he would end up doing a long stretch in prison but on the other hand he was still angry at what this man had done and he felt totally let down by the justice system.

Chambers, in the eyes of the law was now not guilty of killing his wife; he was not responsible for her death in fact the record books would show that Rebecca Reid was the one responsible and that Chambers was the one suffering with the devastating memory of what happened that day.

The more Reid thought about things the more he wanted justice, and as the hours ticked by and Reid sat at home with these thoughts going through his mind he found himself putting on his jacket and climbing into his car then driving over to the address he was given, in what seemed like a blur, Reid was suddenly ringing the door bell and in a matter of seconds later he was being welcomed inside by Karen and shown through to the living room.

Reid had made up his mind and he and Karen began planning what they needed to do to be able to get to the truth. Karen had explained to Reid that she knew there was something strange about the trial and the verdict, she too thought it was to neat and tidy, she told Reid that she no longer had pride in being a police officer and that she had been sickened recently on seeing some nasty and dangerous people walk free from court or receive punishments that didn't fit the crime.

She had taken a few weeks to come to the conclusion that if Chambers was another one who got off or got off lightly that she would look into doing something about it and with Reid's superior army training and his mind set on how the courts had let him down Karen knew that he was the perfect ally in such a caper.

With precision planning they both worked out the times of the prison van would be travelling along that road and how Reid would break chambers out, they also spent a few days watching the movements of the judge and decided the best place to kidnap him was at the pub and they had worked out that this would be done at night and the next morning Reid would break

into Russell's home and hold the three of them hostage there while he waited for police action.

Karen, with her police experience, knew the protocols and what the police would do, she knew that if firearms where involved that the whole neighbourhood would be closed off and a firearms team would be scrambled to the scene also with the threat of explosives being used the whole area would be evacuated which was exactly what Reid needed.

Another important measure was to have Karen involved with the siege in some way, this way she could be working on the inside and relay any information to Reid that he needed to know, this was easy to achieve, all Reid had to do was insist that Detective sergeant Karen Caswell would be present and since she was the officer in charge of the case no one would suspect anything.

They spent a lot of hours working every little detail out even down to having a safe word if they needed to speak to each other, the safe word chosen was Sahara Desert and Karen would slip that into a sentence when talking to Reid if there was some kind of problem during the many and lengthy telephone conversations that Reid would be having with the police.

"It may sound difficult to fit a word like Sahara Desert into a sentence" explained Karen "it has to sound totally natural, but trust me, I can and will find a way of getting it in if I need to, you just have to make sure you hear it" she instructed, Reid reassured her that if the safe word was used at any point he would hear it and act accordingly.

They both knew that they were taking a mighty risk, Karen knew that the law would come down on her with every bit of force it has if she was caught and Reid knew the same, but he felt that he had nothing of value in his life anymore and so had nothing to lose and he knew that if he didn't do something to get justice for his wife's death that it would eat away at him for the rest of his days.

With a fire inside of him which was ignited the second the jury made the wrong decision and an almighty urge to get the truth of what really happened that day, was reason enough for

Reid to be doing this, however he sometimes wondered why Karen would take such a risk.

During one of their breaks from the organising and planning of the siege, Reid decided to ask Karen for her reasons why she was risking everything to help him, they had put many hours in over many days and both felt that they had covered everything, and considered every possible eventuality of anything that could crop up or go wrong, they were aware that they never started with a great deal of time but both Reid and Karen agreed that the plan would work if carried out to the letter.

As they sat in Karen's small but neat and tidy flat which had all the evidence of a female living alone such as flowers, candles and a reasonable collection of romantic comedy box sets, Reid asked yet again what her reasons for doing this where.

The subject had come up before and Karen's reasons where simple, she hated the injustice and she was on this occasion willing to risk everything to put right a massive wrong, but during this moment of down time Reid sat next to her on her cream leather sofa and reached across and held her small pale hand in both of his large strong hands.

And with a serious tone in his voice he again asked the question but on this occasion, it was asked with a certain amount of passion and honesty that Karen recognised as being said by a man who was desperate for an answer that would satisfy him "I know you've told me why you are doing this, and I get it, but what I don't understand is why you're doing this for me? And not for some other poor sucker who has been let down by the courts" Reid asked.

The answer came in a way that Reid never saw coming, when Karen threw caution to the wind and slowly leant forward and placed her soft lips against his, just for a moment Reid's heart fluttered and his arms let go of Karen's hands and he pulled her closer to him with Karen wrapping her arms tightly around his broad frame.

It was at this moment that the gentle kiss turned into a passionate one, but just as quick as the passionate embrace had happened Reid's mind suddenly flooded with memories of his wife, the woman who he was risking everything to get justice for, he pulled away quickly and they were both left sitting inches apart on the sofa with their heads lowered and for a few seconds neither of them spoke. Then at the same time they both said “sorry” they both shared a nervous giggle at this.

And then they did it again as they both began to speak at the same time to explain why it happened, Reid’s voice was the more dominant and his explanation was heard first, “I just feel like I’m cheating on Rebecca, I know that is crazy but it’s true” Karen edged closer to him and placed a reassuring hand on his knee, “I’m the one who should be sorry Steven, not you” she went on to explain “when I first met you I saw a tough and ruggedly handsome ex-soldier who had suffered so much hurt, and as these months have passed and we’ve got to know each other, I have seen beneath all of that and got to know a vulnerable and gentle man, and am afraid my feelings have grown for you, but what just happened was unprofessional of me and it won’t happen again” she said whilst looking deep into Reid’s eyes, Reid acknowledged her explanation with a simple nod of the head.

Reid was attracted to Karen, but any kind of physical relationship wasn't in his plans or his head. He loved his wife and he was existing with a broken heart now that he had lost her, and for him to be risking everything to be able to get justice for her was all he was concerned about.

Both Karen and Reid decided that their focus from that moment on should be and would be on the plan, so they could achieve what they had set out to achieve, so for hour after hour and whenever they had the time they spent it going over exactly what they needed to do, they covered each other's role in the plan and considered every single thing that they thought might occur during the incident.

Until eventually they were both happy and felt that it was all set and ready to go, they knew that they never had a lot of time to prepare for this but what little time they had they used wisely and carefully until they were good to go.

CHAPTER NINE

Reid stood in a shop doorway to take cover from the rain, the corner shop obviously acted as a great convenience to the residents of the few dozen houses that made up the street and it acted as a convenience to Reid right at that moment.

He put his hand into his pocket and pulled out a piece of paper and checked the address written on it against the road sign that was fixed firmly to the front of a house opposite. Once certain that he was at the correct place he began to slowly walk along the narrow-cobbled street passing the small, scruffy looking terraced houses searching for number thirty-two.

After a short while he found himself standing opposite a door with that number written on it in red paint, Reid's initial thought was that the number looked like it had been written by a ten-year-old, but he reminded himself just what kind of area this was and what kind of people lived in a place like this so that could very well be the case.

He saw that there was no bell or a door knocker so Reid gave four reasonably hard knocks onto the door and waited, after a few seconds he saw the hall way light come on through the arched window display of the door and could hear the door being unlocked, it then opened up the few inches the safety chain would allow and he could see half a female face looking out at him, Reid immediately reading the situation as he always did in any encounter had worked out that the female was in her early twenties and judging by the redness to her eyes, lank greasy hair and bad skin that she was either drunk or high.

"I'm looking for Roscoe" said Reid, the girl slowly closed the door and Reid could hear the sound of the door chain being removed then the door was fully opened to reveal the female who was indeed judging by the unsteadiness on her feet was indeed very drunk, she indicated for Reid to step inside which he did and the door was closed behind him, the girl shouted "ROSCOE" at the top of her voice then left the house through the door that Reid had just walked through, leaving Reid standing alone in the hall.

There was no carpet on the floor of the hallway and the stairs to Reid's left where down to the wooden floorboards, A baby gate was in the closed position at the foot of the stairs which made Reid hope to himself that there wasn't a baby being brought up in this place, as it was cold, dirty and many areas where immediately apparent to Reid, where a baby or a child could find themselves getting hurt.

As Reid continued to survey his surroundings he could see clearly that the occupant wasn't much of a cleaner as the skirting boards and what few pieces of furniture the hallway had where all covered with dust, above where Reid was standing was a single low watt light bulb hanging down with no shade and even that had a thick layer of dust covering it.

This was the house of Paul Rossiter, or Roscoe to his friends and associates, a fifty-three-year-old career criminal that had spent his teenage years and his adult life in and out of prison for crimes ranging from burglary, drugs offences, receiving stolen goods and anything that he thought would earn him a quick few quid.

five years previously he had been released from serving half a ten year sentence for manslaughter when he killed a man in a pub car park with a single punch, the fight had been started when Roscoe had heard that the man, who was a known hard man himself, had beaten up his brother in a similar pub fight and Roscoe sought revenge, although he never intended to kill the guy, he did go searching the streets for him before the car park encounter and apparently no words were exchanged between the two as Roscoe simply walked over to him and threw the punch that was to end his life.

Roscoe had been living of that incident ever since and had gained a lot of respect, although through fear, from the other people in the neighbourhood, What the other residents of the area did not know about the legendary hard man was that he was an active police informer and his operational handler was Karen Caswell, she would gather a lot of information from him regarding the activities of some of the local criminals in return for a bit of extra cash and some breathing space from his own small time criminal ventures.

Reid had been waiting in the hallway for a minute or so when he heard a deep voice say "I'm in here", Reid saw a door to his right and wandered through it into a living room which had plumes of smoke hanging in the air from the rolled-up cigarettes that had been smoked in the room, once Reid had become accustomed to the stench of stale tobacco and his eyes had adjusted to the dark murky room and untidy hovel that this man lived in, he saw a large man standing in the corner of the room near a table, which had two drawers on its side.

The man stood well over six-foot-tall, Reid noticed that he stood a few inches taller than himself and was very well built although he was very overweight and his obvious love of food and probably lager had given him a large bell, "Are you Roscoe"? Asked Reid, "Yeah I am, are you Karen's mate"? Was the reply, Reid just nodded in response, On the table where the man stood was a pile of paper work none of which interested Reid, what did interest him was the large padded brown envelope that Roscoe was holding in his right hand, Roscoe threw it towards Reid who caught it without taking his eyes of Roscoe for one second, Reid felt uneasy, not just being in this man's company, but also being in his house and this area, he just wanted to conduct his business as quickly as possible and get out of there.

Reid looked inside the envelope and saw a single passport, the first thing that entered his mind was that the envelope was way too big for what was inside, he tipped the passport out into his hand and checked its authenticity.

Reid had worked a lot of missions over enemy lines in war torn countries and often travelled on fake passports pretending to be someone he wasn't so he knew how a fake passport should look, and he was happy with what he was holding, although he wasn't too pleased with the name written on it, he looked at it for a few seconds then looked up at Roscoe who was watching him expectantly "Gerald Bacon!" he said in an exasperated tone Roscoe smiled back at him and replied "you don't get to choose the names Gerald" Reid never replied, instead he put the passport into the oversized envelope, folded it and placed it into his coat pocket, Roscoe watched as he did this then walked around the side of the table and opened up one of the drawers connected to it, "Are you forgetting something Gerald" he asked, his deep gravelly voice having a sarcastic tone to it.

Reid smirked and nodded and then reached into his other pocket and pulled out an envelope of his own and tossed it onto the table, "the envelope I used is more appropriate" he proudly stated, Roscoe picked it up and quickly counted the bundle of cash inside, after a short while he looked up at Reid with a disappointed expression “it’s light pal” he said dropping the cash on the table, Reid stood firm and replied “four hundred was the deal” Roscoe’s demeanour began to change and Reid noticed this “No, no Gerald, it’s gone up, but just because I like you I’ll let you have it for six hundred instead of the seven hundred I was going to charge you” Reid could feel his heart begin to beat harder and faster and he knew that violence was imminent but as was his usual way he tried to negotiate as he felt it was always better to make things easier rather than take the difficult route.

“Karen said that you had agreed four hundred with her” he pointed out, Roscoe replied with a menacing tone this time as if losing patience, “then she got it fucking wrong, so hand the passport over, go and bring the other two hundred and I’ll give it back to you”.

Reid made a quick assumption that Roscoe was obviously a confident man who thought he could intimidate Reid or if it came down to it that he could beat him in combat. Reid was certain that Roscoe must have weighed him up the second he had saw him, as Reid had done with Roscoe, although Roscoe was the bigger of the two men, Reid wasn't small, and he had age on his side and his physique was a hell of a lot better and he was a lot fitter.

Obviously, Roscoe had no idea of Reid's past history or what he was capable of, if he did it might be a different story, but as it was, Roscoe was brimming with confidence and believed in his own hype that he had the edge over Reid.

As far as Reid was concerned he had been in this stench ridden hovel a lot longer than he intended to and there was no way he was coming back specially to hand over another two hundred pounds that wasn't even part of the deal, he stared straight at Roscoe with a mean look in his eyes and replied "we kept to our side of the bargain, I'm going to leave now, if you want to stop me then there is going to be a problem, a problem that you don't want" Reid said, hoping that the threat would be enough to make Roscoe decide not to engage him.

Reid slowly turned to walk out fully aware and prepared that Roscoe could launch an attack as soon as his back was turned, Roscoe however, had a different solution in mind, he simply reached into the draw he had opened earlier and pulled out a hand gun and pointed it at Reid's back as he turned "Bang bang, you're dead" he said smiling and with a feeling of control.

Reid turned slowly and saw the pistol being pointed at him by the large smiling fat man, it wasn't the first time that Reid had faced down a man, with a gun pointing at him, but he also wasn't stupid, within a second he calculated the distance between himself and Roscoe and he knew there was no way he could get to him and disarm him without a shot being fired so he would have to use his ingenuity on this occasion.

Reid slowly raised his arms in the air and acted as if he was scared for his life "Whoa, okay man, look don't do anything hasty, I'm sure this can all be sorted out" he said with a fake quiver to his voice. He wanted Roscoe's confidence to rise so leading him into a false sense of security, hopefully this would make him, at some point, take his eye off the ball.

With an overwhelming sense of control Roscoe's confidence did just that, it had now risen massively, he walked from behind the table and approached Reid, stopping a couple of meters away from him, with the gun pointing directly at his chest "you can sort it out by organising another two hundred quid" was his confident reply.

Reid, who for the first time, was now closer to Roscoe than he had ever been, immediately took note of the odour of sweat that come from him, his clothing also had the stench of stale cigarette smoke emanating from them which Reid found to be disgusting in a grown man, as the ex-soldier was strict on his appearance and cleanliness.

He thought for a moment and then purposely pulled his mobile phone from his coat pocket very quickly, this made Roscoe react in such a way that Reid quickly had to calm him down "it's just a phone, it's just a phone Roscoe, if I make a quick call I can arrange for the rest of the cash to be brought here in ten minutes" he said hurriedly, "Who are you calling"? Asked Roscoe who was now a little on edge.

Reid replied convincingly and thinking on his feet “a friend of mine, as I said, he will bring the money over then the deal can be done, is that ok”? Reid replied, his quick-thinking brain evaluating the situation all the time.

Roscoe, who was not stupid, as he maintained the couple of meters’ safe distance from Reid, replied “put it on speaker, I want to know who you’re talking too” he ordered, Reid nodded his head and with trembling hands began to fiddle with his mobile, as Roscoe looked on, Reid purposely fumbled with the phone and started to lose his cool pretending that he was having trouble getting the phone onto speaker mode, with sweaty hands and his breathing becoming quick and shallow with apparent fear, he began to swear at the phone in his hand and acted like a man whose life was in the balance.

This went on for half a minute with Reid acting like a petrified man who couldn't get to grips with the technology of his phone, in reality, Reid was waiting for Roscoe's attention to be shifted just a little, with the distraction he was creating.

He wanted Roscoe's attention to move from the gun he had pointing at his chest to the antics now going on opposite him with this shaking scared man and his phone, at the precise moment that Reid believed he had a split second window to act, he took it by throwing the phone very quick and hard into the face of Roscoe, even before Roscoe could flinch and react to the phone smashing into his face, Reid had moved forward with cat like reflexes, the couple of meters' distance between the two, that Roscoe was protecting, had gone, and as soon as he was in striking distance Reid connected with a right hook that was delivered with such power, Roscoe's legs crumbled beneath him and he collapsed to the floor, Reid followed the punch with a right knee to the face as he grabbed hold of

Roscoe's right hand twisting it round consequently making him release his grip on the pistol.

Reid took hold of the gun and pistol-whipped Roscoe twice more to the head rendering him unconscious. When Roscoe began to regain consciousness again, and being totally unaware of how long he'd been out for, he felt immense pain to his head and blood from a large wound on his forehead was running into his right eye causing it to sting and unable to see out of.

He knew he was laid on the floor and attempted to get to his feet, but it was at this point he realised that Reid had used the speaker cables, pulled from his old stereo system that occupied a dark corner of the room, to bind his arms and feet.

As he lay on the floor struggling with the ties he heard Reid's voice above him "I've just been on the phone to Karen and I'm afraid she isn't very pleased that you tried to rip us off" he said, Roscoe momentarily stopped fidgeting with the ties when he heard Reid's voice.

"she said you can expect every person, in this shit hole of a neighbourhood, to know that you are a police grass within an hour". He informed a now worried Roscoe, who sank his head into the dirty stained carpet upon hearing the news.

Reid had filled his pockets with the four hundred pounds that had been thrown onto the table and was about to leave, but he gave one last kick to the flabby body of Roscoe before he started to walk away, which left him gasping for breath, the blood from his head wound leaving more stains on the only carpet in the house.

As Reid left the room and opened up the front door he turned one last time and shouted out so Roscoe could hear “if I was you, I’d try to get out of those ties and get the fuck out of this house as quick as you can, before the locals find out you’re a snitch and burn this place down with you in it” Reid then turned and left the house slamming the door behind him, he then walked slowly away back in the direction he came from with his shoulders hunched up to protect himself from the rain.

When Reid had returned to Karen’s apartment he was soaked through to the skin, cold and the incident at Roscoe’s place hadn’t left him in a great mood.

When the door was opened Karen greeted him with a smile and let him enter, Reid never smiled back instead he immediately went into a tirade of abuse about what had just happened “I thought you said that this guy was cool” he said.

“He’s never been a problem in the past, I suppose I just never realised what an idiot he also is” Karen replied, wanting to steady Reid’s mood, they both made their way to the living room where Karen had the radiators on full and Reid could feel the wall of heat as he entered, he let out a sigh of satisfaction as he felt the warmth on his body and took off his rain soaked coat and hung it across one of the radiators.

He then took out the passport from his pocket and the four hundred in cash and threw both items onto the small coffee table, Karen immediately picked up the passport to inspect it “you wouldn’t know it’s a fake” she remarked, “Are you happy with the photo I passed onto him”? She asked.

Reid replied with a touch of disdain “the photo is fine, the name isn’t” he said, Karen took a quick look and on seeing the name Gerald Bacon she gave a sly smile “it suits you, Gerald” she replied.

“Careful” said Reid “the last person who called me Gerald, ended up laying in a pool of his own blood” he said playfully, this comment lightened the mood a little and made Karen laugh out loud “it’s ok for you” Reid commented, “after all this is finished I’ve got to spend the rest of my days being called Gerald fucking Bacon” he said somewhat humorously.

Karen smiled “you have a middle name as well I see” she replied with a sharp wit, both Reid and Karen shared a laugh at her joke, and it was only then that Reid felt the relief he always felt after a successful operation was over.

While Karen made them both a hot drink, Reid made himself comfortable by taking off his soaked training shoes, the rain had passed right through the fabric of shoes, soaking Reid's socks, which he placed onto the radiator to dry off.

After his clothing was all removed and was drying on the radiators and Reid was wearing the dressing gown Karen had provided, he began to finally warm himself using the electric fire which had been turned on to full power, picking up a foot stool and sitting opposite it, he rubbed his hands together as he enjoyed the heat and being dry.

As he did this Karen shouted through from the kitchen "I've made a few relevant phone calls and it's safe to say that what Roscoe attempted to do tonight, he will regret for the rest of his life" she said with a great deal of satisfaction. "Let's put it this way, he should move out of that area tonight because by the morning every person on that estate will know what he is" she explained to a grinning Reid.

Karen brought in two cups of tea, placed Reid's cup on the table and sat down on the sofa with hers, Reid picked up his cup and joined Karen on the sofa. With the passport in Reid's possession and an extra four hundred pounds in cash, everything was now in place, all they had to do now was carry out what they had been planning for.

CHAPTER TEN

Over an hour had passed in the cellar and Reid, along with his three hostages were wondering why they had heard nothing from the police who had taken up residence outside. Reid knew they had, as he was fortunate to have the use of a small eight-inch square window, which on the outside of the house was at ground level, there was six windows like it, spaced out a foot apart, and their function was to provide some natural light into the cellar.

A couple of them where positioned so they provided a perfect view of the main gates and Reid could see the police where in full attendance, He had spent the last several minutes looking at his phone, checking the battery had enough power and checking that he had a signal, both of which he had, with over eighty percent power and a full five bars of signal, he was now wondering why no one had called.

His mind began to wander, had Mrs. Bilton Russell given the police the mobile number on the piece of paper he had handed her? maybe she had lost it, meaning the police had no method of contact, or maybe he had written down the wrong number and

hadn't noticed, or where the police playing mind games and letting him sweat for a while, he thought to himself that if that was the case, it was a very risky tactic to use especially since he was holding three hostages at gun point.

Reid suddenly snapped himself out of the negative mind set he put himself into and remembered that in order to succeed in such situations that he must have complete control of his mind and thoughts.

Everything had been planned down to the finest detail and every possible problem had been looked at and a solution was in place if such a problem should arise, he back tracked with his thoughts, of course he hadn't written down the wrong number he wouldn't be that careless and of course Mrs Bilton Russell had handed over the piece of paper, her husband's life depended on it, so whatever the reason was that the police where taking so long to call it wasn't anything that was down to him.

Suddenly, as the four men sat in silence, with the only sound being heard was the bird song coming from the garden above them, the silence was broken, as Reid's phone burst into life, the ring tone of a traditional phone ringing was set to the highest volume and it made the three hostages flinch when it started to ring, Reid however remained stony faced and never flinched a bit, his nerves of steel on show for the others to see.

Reid calmly pressed the answer key and spoke “who am I speaking to”? He asked, “I am inspector Jo Tucker” came the reply “I’m the officer in charge, what do I call you”? asked Tucker, “You can call me Steven or just Reid, chief Inspector but I’ll have to correct you on one small detail” he replied with authority, there was a second’s pause before Tucker spoke “what is that Steven”? she asked, Reid spoke calmly and slowly with a hint of menace to his voice “You’re not the one in charge, I am” again there was a second’s pause that Reid had left purposely to enhance the tension that was building “is that clear chief inspector”? He continued.

Tucker, who had acted as negotiator on many occasions with incidents such as these, remembered the first rule of hostage negotiations, and that was to build a rapport with the hostage taker, “clear as Chrystal Steven” Tucker immediately replied, getting herself into negotiator mode right from the off.

It was obviously difficult to begin to build a rapport when Tucker knew nothing about the person she was talking to so the best way to try and win someone over was to be friendly and use humour.

Tucker wasn’t known for her comedic prowess, but she knew all the tricks and she felt that she could hold a conversation with Reid and control the situation, what she needed to do was get Reid talking and make him feel relaxed whilst talking to her.

“since you’re unable to get my rank correct” Tucker said, while smiling down the phone, hoping that Reid would pick up on the humorous way her comment was intended “you’ve just promoted me, so thank you for that”, why don’t you just call me by my name? Which is Jo” she said, “that’s if you would prefer it that way?” she added confidently.

With the help of Karen, Reid had studied the police protocol of handling situations such as this and was very familiar with the strategy being used by Tucker and he was happy to oblige with the rapport building “that is fine by me Jo” he said, “if building a rapport with me makes you easier to deal with then so be it, now shall we get down to business” he said with an air of cockiness.

Tucker however, was happy to let Reid take the lead and she would happily let him think that he was in complete control, she saw these kind of incidents as a chess game, she always believed that it was her intelligence and logical thinking along with the tried and tested tactics that the police employ against her opponent's tactics and mind power.

And she didn't see this incident being any different, even without knowing any of the facts about Reid or whoever he had taken as a hostage or the reasons for why Reid had done this, Tucker was going to play it in the same way she always had done.

She was supremely confident that no matter how long it took, she would be making an arrest at the end of it and any hostage would be freed unharmed, that was always the case in the past and she knew the rule book inside out, back to front and upside down, so she had no doubt that the same outcome would happen on this occasion.

The basic strategy was to seem to be doing all she can to follow the instructions of the hostage taker, certain requests are carried out without any problems, if they ask for food to be brought in, then they get it, if they wish to be in contact with someone then they will be, Tucker knew that her aim was to keep Reid happy if she could, but before anything could begin she needed to know that Russell was alive and well and unharmed, so she started by asking Reid about Russell.

"Before we go any further Steven, I'm sure you will understand, that I need to be sure if Mr Bilton Russell is safe and well" Tucker asked politely "I have a very distraught Mrs Bilton Russell here and I'd like to give her some good news" she added, Reid again knew that as long as the police where fully aware that the hostages where safe and well then, he had bargaining power as well as control, so he was pleased to answer Tuckers question, the answer she received from Reid ended up leaving Tucker surprised and having to re-evaluate her tactics.

“All the hostages are fine, apart from a few cuts and grazes but nothing else I can assure you of that” he replied, Tucker looked at her sergeant with a confused expression, she was only aware of one hostage, so she was very eager to know of anyone else that Reid Was holding.

“All the hostages?” she asked, with a shocked expression on her face, for everyone present inside the command centre to see, Reid smiled to himself as he realised that Tucker and the police where not in possession of the full facts. “yes, all of them” replied Reid, with a feeling of satisfaction.

This new piece of information now left Tucker with more work to do and in a tricky position, she simply had to find out how many hostages they were and who they were and also how and when Reid had taken them hostage "How many are you holding Steven?" quizzed Tucker, Reid, still smiling at having one over the police, proudly explained "three, I have Craig Chambers who I sprung from a prison van yesterday morning and Judge Brian Pengilly who never made it home from his local pub last night, and you know about Oliver, I take it you're not aware of this Jo?" Reid asked.

Tucker hit the mute button on the speaker phone and instructed her officers to make some checks about what she and the other officers present where just informed of, she then went back to talking to Reid "You're absolutely correct Steven, I had no idea of the other two" she explained.

Reid moved the phone from his ear and put it onto loud speaker mode and placed it down onto the work bench, he then sat down near it and looked at the three men as he spoke, "don't you people talk to each other?" he asked, Jo went straight onto the defensive "well to be fair, we cannot make any connections between crimes until we have all the facts, how are we supposed to know that the escape of a prisoner and the kidnapping of an elderly judge were all connected to you and Bilton Russell?" she declared, fighting her corner.

"fair point I suppose, but you know now, so go and do any checks that you need to and then call me back, however before you do that I want you to get someone for me" announced Reid sternly.

Reid needed his inside man, or on this occasion, inside woman, and he needed Karen there right at the start, Karen had put all this together and without her working on the other side and feeding him with information of what the police where planning on doing the whole thing would be a lot more difficult.

Jo replied with her tactics at the forefront of her mind "who is that Steven?" she asked, Reid as was part of the plan instructed Tucker to get hold of Sergeant Karen Caswell, he explained that he would only deal with her and no one else.

The name didn't mean anything to Tucker so she was inquisitive to who she was and why she was so imperative to Reid, "I can try and locate this person for you Steven, but you can't blame me for wanting to know why you want her and why you'll only speak to her" explained Tucker, Reid had anticipated such a question “you will find out everything you need to know in due course” he replied, this left tucker with an unanswered question which is something she didn’t like, but as the protocol dictates she knew she had to follow it and find Caswell if she was ever going to get to the bottom of what Reid was up to.

This first contact with Reid had thrown Tucker off balance a bit, initially with finding out that there were two more hostages than she expected and then finding out that Reid was planning on talking to another officer and not her.

For Reid though, having the police off balance is what he wanted, and his aim was to try and maintain their lack of equilibrium throughout the siege, Tuckers aim in this, was to get herself settled and begin to deal with the situation in such a way where she could see things coming and have no more surprises.

CHAPTER ELEVEN

Tucker had delegated the tasks of finding out all they can about the prison break of Chambers and the kidnapping of Pengilly to some of her trusted officers. she had decided to concentrate on finding Karen caswell herself, as she was intrigued to know what she was to Reid and why Reid was so determined to have her present.

After a phone call to the police station, Tucker had been informed that Karen had been contacted and was on her way the scene, Tucker liked to be in control, and at this moment she had handed over control of the situation to Reid, but she knew that this was only a temporary measure, and it was all part of the negotiation strategy.

But she was concerned about how much control Reid was expecting Karen to have, Tucker was the officer in charge, no matter what Reid thought, and she had decades' worth of experience and she was going to control this incident as it was her duty to do so, and she knew that no one could do it better than she could.

She was very eager to talk to Karen and make it clear that if the situation arises and Reid insists that Karen is the lead negotiator, then Tucker would be running the show from behind the scenes without Reid being aware of it.

In the cellar, things where not moving forward as fast as Russell would have liked, Reid seemed relaxed and was prepared to wait for however long things took, but Russell was quite an impatient man who never liked waiting around for anything and never had, and even though on this occasion he was being held against his will and tied to a table, he still found it a challenge to hold his tongue, and after stewing for such a long time, he was finding it more and more difficult not to voice his disapproval of the situation.

he tried so hard to keep quiet, but the longer he sat there the more the situation began to irritate him, until eventually the simplest of things where winding him up, the one thing that could easily make him blow at this point was the silence, all four men just sat still and without a sound, and it total silence that Russell found to be so annoying, especially as he could hear Chambers breathing through his nose, the sound of

the shallow shaky breaths of the scared Chambers were getting on Russell's nerves more and more by the second.

there was the odd noise from outside that found its way into the cellar and the ticking of Reid's watch seemed to be amplified by the quietness, even the creaking of the chair, when Pengilly adjusted his position every few minutes, annoyed Russell, and he began showing his aggravation by flashing Pengilly the odd look of disapproval coupled with some long drawn out sighs and shakes of the head.

This had little effect on Pengilly, he was an elderly man who found it difficult to get comfortable at the best of times never mind being sat on a hard-plastic folding chair for hours with his hands fastened to a table like they were.

Chambers had other problems as he was beginning to feel the effects of drug withdrawal, and with no medical examiner to administer methadone to ease his discomfort, his anguish was plain to see, his skin was beginning to pour with sweat, some of which ran from his forehead down into his eyes, which caused them to sting and without being able to wipe it away

with his hand he had to move his head to his arms to wipe the sweat away, the way the cables fastened his arms to the table made this simple task difficult to do.

Another way to counter act this problem was to flick his head from side to side quickly and vigorously so to let the sweat fly off his head and his hair, this however was met with anger by Russell as he felt some of the sweat land on him, with every fibre of his being Russell wanted to scream in Chambers' face to stop.

In Russell's mind he pictured Chambers shaking the sweat from his head like a dog shaking the water from its coat when in reality it wasn't anything like that but everything that irritated Russell seemed to be magnified tenfold.

Chambers' breathing was starting to become erratic, and he found it impossible to control some of the muscle tremors that would make his legs twitch and his shoulders flinch involuntarily, this caught the attention of Pengilly who looked across at chambers with concern.

Pengilly looked over at Reid, who had taken this moment of down time to rest; he was leant back on his chair with his eyes closed and his body seemed limp and relaxed, to the eye he could pass for being asleep, but Reid was able to rest without actually sleeping and had done so many times before at times when sleeping could mean you put your own and other people's lives in danger.

Pengilly however was concerned for chambers to such an extent that he decided to speak up, "I don't think he's very well" he said directing his concerns towards Reid, who simply opened one eye and took a quick look at Chambers "he'll be ok" he answered before closing his eye again and returning to his relaxed state.

The judge never shared Reid's opinion and again voiced his concerns "look at him, he's obviously not ok" he said this time in a more alarmed way, Reid this time opened up both eyes, took a quick look at Chambers then switched his gaze over to the judge, "it's called drug withdrawal judge, he isn't going to die" explained Reid in a none caring fashion, then closed his eyes again.

The judge responded as if proving a point "he isn't on drugs anymore, he has been on a rehab course so has kicked the habit, you should remember that from the court case" he proudly announced, Reid opened his eyes wide with astonishment, raised his eyebrows and gave out a dramatic fake laugh to enhance his point, without a word being said by Reid he got his point over to the judge loud and clear.

The judge thought for a second, his expression visibly changing as it suddenly dawned on him that he had been lied to in his court room, he took a look to his left where Russell was sitting staring straight ahead, "that statement was made under oath" said Pengilly with a shocked tone Russell slowly turned to face Pengilly "do you honestly think that matters now?" he said before turning to face forwards again, this gave Reid the ideal opportunity to speak his mind "you see Judge, even in a court of law and under oath, people will say what they need to say in order to get what they want, I'm very surprised however that this is news to you" Reid announced, Pengilly looked disappointed, "it is news to me, and I'm appalled, of course I'm aware that lies are often told in court, but I never thought they would be told by barristers, and especially not by you Mr Bilton Russell, a man of such high standing" said Pengilly,

Reid interjected with his opinion "you'll find by the end of all this, that he's lied about more than just a drugs rehab Judge, you wait and see" he said with a smile and a wink that was directed towards Russell who never reacted, he stared straight ahead, and his face was set in an emotionless expression as he fought hard to keep his counsel and hold his temper.

Reid couldn't leave it there, he saw this as an opportunity to air some of his views, so grabbed it with both hands "if he's lied about the drugs rehab judge, imagine what else he's lied about" Reid said, goading Russell or Pengilly or both into a reaction "and in your courtroom too" he added sarcastically.

Neither Russell or pengilly made a comment, both men recognising that Reid was using the subject to press a few buttons and taunt them both, as Reid spoke both men remained silent and avoided looking at him.

This never stopped Reid from continuing however “do you think that Chambers’ entire defence was a lie? maybe it’s all lies, and we are going to find that out today, here, In the cellar of this beautiful house” Reid said while still sitting slouched back on his chair, with his eyes now closed again, only opening them once in a while to gauge any reaction he may be getting.

Even though there was nothing coming back from either man, Reid was clever enough to know that his words where hitting home and internally at least one if not both men where seething, and where desperately wanting to say something in defence, he felt that any reaction from this moment might not be made apparent now, but could possibly manifest itself later on in some way, so he happily continued.

“just imagine if this house has been bought on lies” Reid carried on saying, speaking slowly to enhance his point “imagine if his entire career has been running on lies, if that’s the case, and it’s a good chance it could be, imagine how many dangerous criminals are walking the streets right now, because of his lies” Reid said, enjoying every single word as he said it.

With still no reaction from either man, Reid smiled to himself and decided to leave it there, he settled back into an even comfier position, satisfied having had that impromptu moment that he felt he used to great effect.

Reid had a good idea, but couldn’t be certain, that his words had made Russell or Pengilly angry or upset in some way, which is what he wanted to achieve at that moment. He was good at reading human emotion and with a quick study of the micro expressions of both men, Reid considered his spoken observations had, had the desired effect, as he observed both of them he noticed the bitter and angry look of Russell's expression, that he was attempting to suppress and Pengilly with a look of great disappointment and frustration that was painted all over his face.

With a smile and a nod to himself of satisfaction, Reid closed his eyes again and settled back to rest for however long he had until his phone rang.

Pengilly and Russell where both left with their own thoughts whirring around in their heads, with neither man wanting to voice their opinions. Russell, although he wanted to, did not allow himself to defend his status, especially not to Reid who Russell saw as a common criminal, so he convinced himself that he never had anything to prove to such a low life.

Instead he went back to listening to the silence and observing the annoying mannerisms of his fellow hostages, and found that fighting to control his frustrations and irritabilities actually helped him to cope in a strange way.

Things where moving very slowly and like Reid obviously had, Russell was trying to come to terms with the fact that they were going to be waiting for a lot of hours, and there was nothing that could be done to make it go quicker, so he simply had to sit and wait, and expect to be waiting for a long time.

With a few deep breaths, for composure, Russell tried to relax his shoulders and prepared himself for the wait, until the phone rang, and things would move

CHAPTER TWELVE

Tucker had called in the officer in charge of the firearms team, code named silver command. They both stood at one quiet end of the command centre and where discussing the situation, tuckers main concerns where obviously the safety of the three hostages and a plan was needed should the firearms team had to move in.

The man in charge of the team was a rugged man in his mid-forties, he was of average height and build and his name was Sergeant Ian Danks, he had over a decade's experience as an armed police officer and his knowledge was of value to Tucker, she had zero intentions of making any significant moves at this point, but she wanted to have the opinion of someone of Danks experience.

The opinion of Danks was that in most cases of an armed siege they usually end with the gunman surrendering which is the outcome that Tucker preferred, the not so preferable outcome was that the firearms team would have to move in, this would complicate things, Danks insisted on getting the plans of the house so he and his team could scrutinise it and plan an assault if one should be necessary.

What concerned Danks and tucker at this stage was that even though the house was being watched from the front by armed officers and the CCTV cameras of the mobile command centre, and they also had several armed officers positioned amongst the trees at the rear of the house, no one had seen any movement from within the house, Tucker remembered what Mrs Bilton Russell had told her, that Reid had got her to open the cellar door, which she had done.

This lead Tucker to think that Reid was holding the three men down in the cellar and the house itself was empty and not being used, this made good hearing for Danks as he knew if this was correct that his men could gain entry to the house without Reid's knowledge should they have to.

But for the time being these where plans that Tucker was hoping she would not have to adopt and her main focus was on getting all three men out unharmed and Reid into custody, to do that she needed to negotiate, so she decided that while she waited for the arrival of Karen Caswell she would give Reid a call and try to find out a bit more about the person she considered was her opponent.

Tucker dialled Reid's number as Danks exited the command centre. She sat behind the desk waiting for him to answer, the phone rang three times, when it was answered by Reid with a simple “go ahead” in a deep throaty voice, like a man who had just been disturbed from relaxing.

Tucker started off with some pleasantries, wanting to keep Reid’s mood high “Hi Steven, its Jo Tucker, is everything ok over there, is there anything you need?” she asked politely and in high spirits hoping her mood would be infectious enough for Reid to follow suit.

Reid, who as usual, had the phone on speaker, never answered Tuckers questions but instead came back with one of his own, “Has Karen arrived?” he asked bluntly, Tucker explained that she hadn’t but that she was on her way, and that she was just making sure all was well and if he needed anything.

Reid felt that this phone call was a complete waste of time so simply hung up the phone without saying anything else, Tucker sat and listened to the purring sound of a line which had just been disconnected and with a somewhat stunned expression on her face, she placed the phone back on the receiver and looked up at her staff, “it seems we won’t be talking to him until Miss Caswell arrives” she said.

She picked up a radio and with it held at chest level she called her sergeant who she had sent to pick up Caswell from the station “DI Tucker to detective Constable Fogarty, receiving over” she said and waited for a reply, it came within seconds “Go ahead Ma’am” was the reply.

“I take it you’ve collected Sergeant Caswell” said Tucker “that’s affirmative ma’am” replied Fogarty, Tucker looked at her watch, it had been a little over an hour since she had sent

Fogarty to collect Caswell from the station and she was starting to feel a little redundant as she knew Steven was not willing to speak to her, she wanted to get things moving and at present things where standing still and Tucker didn't like it "I need an ETA" she said in hope that it wouldn't be too long, she waited for a reply staring at the radio, willing the answer to arrive quickly.

After thirty seconds had passed which to Tucker felt like several minutes her radio crackled into life with the reply she was waiting for "should be with you in about twenty minutes the traffic isn't to good" fogarty explained.

Tucker was relieved, twenty minutes wasn't ideal, but it wasn't too bad either, she could hold for twenty minutes, then she would brief Caswell on what was happening which would take approximately ten minutes and she would orchestrate things within half an hour.

Tucker replied to Fogarty asking him to make it quicker if possible and then went and sat at her desk, not sure what to do next, just as she sat down her sergeant walked in with the news she had been waiting for on the other kidnap victims.

Sergeant Grey had worked with Tucker on many occasions and she liked his work ethic so much that she always made sure that he was part of any team that she put together, He had many years' experience and also enjoyed the big cases that Tucker had him working on.

He was as disappointed as Tucker was about losing out on the kidnap case of Lauren Harley, but he felt it had been replaced by another, even more interesting one and he felt this because he had done some research on the hostages.

As Grey approached an expectant Tucker he couldn't help give a smile "I've found out who our two other hostages are Jo" he said with an excitable tone, Tucker invited him to sit which he did, opposite her, and they spoke across the table from each other, "Craig Chambers was a serving prisoner, doing an eighteen months stretch for vehicle theft, he'd just appeared in court that morning for an unconnected offence and was being taken back to prison when the van that was transporting him was hijacked by a large I.C one male armed with a handgun" Tucker sat in silence taking it all in with an interested look on her face, "Go on" she replied, Grey continued "A mister Brian Pengilly, never returned home from his regular Friday night drink at his local, his family reported him missing to police and during investigations made, it became known that he was taken by force, and bundled into the back of a white transit van",

Tucker immediately spun around in her seat and started to operate the mouse that controlled the CCTV, she moved one of the cameras and zoomed into the vehicles that stood on the driveway, she zoomed in on a white transit van until it filled the screen, then turned and looked at Grey “a white van, just like that one?” she said.

Grey nodded with a smile, before he carried on “it seems that on the night Pengilly was snatched, our kidnapper had an altercation with three men in the car park of the pub, they caught him hiding in the bushes and had words with him, but our man wasn’t much of a talker and assaulted the shit out of the three of them” said Grey.

Tucker again looked on as Grey spoke, taking in all the information “was there a description?” she asked, “yes there was, if you could call it that” replied Grey “A white male, large build, was all they had" Grey answered, sounding a little embarrassed with the lack of description that he had to offer.

Tucker with a hint of disappointment sat back in her seat "is that it?" She asked, "They obviously got pretty close, for him to assault the three of them and that's the best description they have" she commented, Grey nodded in disbelief "All three went to hospital, one had a broken nose, one had a fractured cheek bone and several missing teeth and another had his jaw broken, maybe it affected their memory" he said.

Tucker sat quiet for a short while thinking, "if it is our guy sat in there with three hostages, I want to know for what reason he has taken these guys" she said, she rose from her chair and stood near the window and looked out towards the house, Grey stood also and stood beside her.

“This was planned, the prison van escape, loitering around in pub car parks in the dead of night, and walking into the house of a top barrister armed with a pistol, but for what reason?” said Tucker, she glanced over at Grey “Why are the three connected?” she asked, Grey never replied but kept looking towards the house.

Tucker walked towards the part of the mobile incident unit that had tea and coffee making facilities, she checked the water level in the kettle and switched it on “I’m hoping Karen Caswell can supply the answer to that when she eventually arrives” remarked Tucker “in the meantime, we’re left to wonder what connects the dots” she said as she poured herself a hot drink and sat back down at her desk.

Tucker was fighting the frustration of waiting for Karen to arrive, but there was nothing she could do other than wait, she now had more information, but she was still left with unanswered questions, some of which she never had earlier.

As they waited Tucker and Grey sat watching the CCTV monitors that covered the front of the house and chatted, Tucker felt that she couldn't fully work out her strategy because there was still gaps in her knowledge of the situation.

Tucker liked to have things prepared so she was ready to go when she needed to, but the thought that was running through her head and which was bothering her was that when Karen finally arrives and if she can fill in the gaps that Tucker had, they will then have to get on the phones and begin negotiating immediately.

Too much time has been wasted already, which meant that Tucker would have had very little time to prepare and this was a concern, however she knew that she had the experience and the skills to be able to deal with times such as this and would simply have to on this occasion.

Tucker must have checked her watch a dozen times in the space of five minutes, and every minute or so she would glance out of the window toward the outer cordon to see if Fogarty was pulling up in the car, it was obvious to Grey and to Tucker herself that the waiting was becoming tiresome and she was itching to get some dialogue going with Reid.

With every minute that ticked by, Tucker felt it was valuable time lost that she could have spent preparing, and also time lost when negotiations could have been taking place, in the pit of her stomach she could feel her frustration growing.

CHAPTER THIRTEEN

It was of course inevitable that at some point during the siege that toilet issues would arise, and Reid knew this only too well, his plan was to wait until someone needed the toilet and he had a way of dealing with it, he himself needed to go but he could hold it in for hours at a time and he didn't want the others to know or think about the toilet otherwise they would all want to go, even though it could be done safely, he never wanted to have to sort out toilet visits until it was absolutely necessary, so he had sat for over half an hour needing to pee but had said and done nothing about it.

It came as no surprise then that it was the oldest of the group who needed to go and spoke out first "I'm afraid I need to use the toilet old boy" said the judge as if talking to an old friend.

Reid glanced up at Pengilly from his seated position and although it was expected, the judges request was met with a sigh "unless you expect me to do it while sitting here" said Pengilly. Reid slowly rose from his seat and walked towards a tool box which was sitting on the floor near the wall.

He opened it, and the others could hear the movement of objects within the box as Reid searched for the item he was looking for, after a little while Reid stood up proudly with a pair of secateurs in his right hand, he approached the bench were all three men sat and walked around the back of it and stood behind the judge placing both hands onto his shoulders "Okay, this is how this works" said Reid in an instructive tone "while I take the judge to the lav, you two just sit quiet and don't try anything, is that clear?" instructed Reid Chambers and Russell never answered and just sat facing forward, which annoyed Reid "I'm not talking to my fucking self-gentlemen" Reid announced in a raised voice, this made Russell turn to face Reid and he nodded his head quickly, Reid then waited from some reaction from Chambers which never came, Reid moved from behind the judge by taking one large step to his left until he stood directly behind Chambers, he slapped chambers hard across the back of the head, "Are you deaf or just ignoring me?" he said, Chambers reacted to the slap with a yelp of pain and then said in a flustered manner that he had heard Reid and that he would do as he was told.

This was good enough for Reid who then returned to standing behind the judge, he leant over and cut off the judge's cable ties with the secateurs, he placed the cutters on the table

and helped the judge to his feet by grabbing his arms and leading him around the table and towards the stairs, he stopped on the way to pick up the mobile phone and with gun in hand he began to march the judge step by step up the stairs towards the door, he gave a look towards Chambers and Russell as they walked, and they just stared back at him with a nervousness about them.

As they reached the top of the stairs, Reid instructed Pengilly to unlock the door with the key that hung in the lock and they both left the cellar and out into the hallway to the house with Reid holding the pistol at Pengilly at all times.

The toilet was one of three in the house, the other two where situated upstairs, the one Reid would be using was only two doors down from the cellar door, as the judge entered the small toilet, Reid stood outside and waited, the judge turned to close the door but Reid put his hand on it preventing him from doing so, this annoyed Pengilly "give me a bit of privacy will you please" he asked in an abrupt manner "no chance judge, I want to see you at all times" came the reply from Reid, just as abruptly.

Pengilly was offended at the very thought of urinating with another man watching and voiced his concerns “now look here my good man, I don’t know what you think I can get up to in this small room, but remember I’m an elderly man, I haven’t eaten in many hours and I’ve not slept, and you’ve had me tied up in a cold cellar, so I’m not going to allow you to degrade me any further” he said sternly.

Reid looked intensely at Pengilly “you either go with the door open or you don’t go at all” said Reid, meaning every word, the judge could tell that Reid meant it and with a moan of disapproval he turned to face the toilet and the door was left open as Reid stood guard outside and left the judge to do his business.

Back down in the cellar, Chambers and Russell where sat quietly and could hear the mutterings of read and Pengilly from upstairs, as Chambers sat with his head down, the affects from his drug withdrawal becoming worse by every passing hour, Russell had made a startling discovery, he had noticed the cutters that Reid had used to free Pengilly had been left on the work bench about a foot away from where he sat.

He sat and stared at them for a moment then looked at Chambers to alert him of their presence "Hey, look" he said, Chambers lifted his head and followed Russell as he directed him with his head towards where the secateurs where laying.

When Chambers saw them he immediately looked back at Russell "No don't touch them, he'll kill us" he said, Russell didn't agree "if you think any of us are getting out of here alive, you're a moron" he barked back at Chambers.

Chambers didn't answer so Russell carried on "this is our chance to get out of here, and if I'm presented with a chance then I take it" he explained, as they sat there and not knowing how much time they had Russell went to work, leaning over to his right as far as he could, the cable ties cutting into his wrists as he manoeuvred his body as far over to the right as possible, the further he leant over the deeper they cut into his skin, he felt the stinging pain this was causing but all he could think about was freedom and safety.

Eventually he managed to make contact with the cutters with his forehead and could just manage to move them closer bit by bit towards himself, all the time he was listening out to any sounds that he could hear upstairs, as Russell managed to edge the cutters a bit closer each time it started to become a bit easier and a bit less painful for him, every so often he would stop and listen when he heard sounds from the hallway of his house.

Upstairs in the toilet Reid was becoming increasingly concerned with the amount of time Pengilly was taking "Jesus Christ Judge, will you hurry up" he said loudly, the judge gave him a look over his shoulder as he stood facing the toilet, "it's not my fault, you're making me nervous, I've never had to urinate at gun point before" replied Pengilly "Really? I've done it many times myself" said Reid, "if you would just close the door I'm sure I'd be more relaxed" Pengilly suggested, Reid was beginning to become frustrated again "the door stays open, you're not a child, now either piss or we go back downstairs" was the order from Reid.

As Reid was becoming frustrated with Pengilly upstairs, Russell was downstairs carrying out his plan to escape which had just dropped into his lap, he had now managed to get the secateurs into his teeth and he passed them into his hands, all this was under the watchful eye of Chambers, who along with the withdrawal from the drugs that he was experiencing he was now on edge as he watched Russell trying to cut himself free.

Russell was fiddling around with the cutters trying to get them into a position so he could snip away at the ties, it seemed to take an age and Chambers' heart felt like it was in his mouth as he watched on, eventually and with some skilful manoeuvring of the cutters, Russell was able to start cutting the plastic ties a bit at a time until he then cut through one of the ties which made it easier as he freed one hand then another, within seconds he had also cut Chambers free and they were both on their feet wondering what their next move should be.

Russell began looking around the cellar telling Chambers to arm himself, Chambers on hearing this froze on the spot with fear, Russell noticed that his unlikely ally was petrified and grabbed him by both his shoulders "listen, there is only one way out of here, and that's up the stairs" he said sharply "now when he comes through the door, we'll be waiting at the top of the stairs to hit him with something hard, and we keep hitting him until he doesn't move anymore" Russell explained to a frightened Chambers who stared wildly back at him.

Chambers heard what Russell was saying and deep down he knew that it was their only chance of escape, but he could not get over the fear "what if we fail? he has a gun and he's a hard bastard" Chambers pointed out.

Russell, conscious of the lack of time available tried one last time to get Chambers on side "this is our only chance, otherwise we die down here, today, now grab something big heavy and hard and make it quick" he said, Russell ran straight to a tool box and fished around inside for a few seconds then produced an oversized spanner, which would do a considerable amount of damage if it was used to hit someone with, when he turned around he saw Chambers holding a bottle of his expensive wine, he was hitting it into the palm of his hand as if to check it for weight, he looked up at Russell “what about this?” he asked, Russell had a look of horror on his face “no way, put it back, that’s worth a fortune, plus we want to render him unconscious not get him pissed” he replied, as he kicked a hammer in the direction of Chambers that he saw lying on the floor. Both men, now armed, ran to the top of the stairs and stood in silence on the three-foot square bit of landing that the stairway provided, waiting for the door to open, Chambers’ heart was beating so fast and loud that he could hear it himself and he was sweating and shaking and finding it difficult to breath, it wasn’t just through fear that was causing Chambers to hyperventilate and shake but also the withdrawal symptoms that was now beginning to consume his body and with the passing of time, was beginning to control his movements and thoughts.

Russell tried to formulate a plan for them to follow, he knew that he would have to be the one to take control of this situation that he had started, he could only hope that Chambers could deliver when the time came.

"As soon as he steps through the door we both start swinging at him, and don't stop, is that understood?" Russell said in hushed tones, Chambers holding the hammer with sweaty palms wasn't sure "what if the old guy comes through first?" he asked.

"He probably will, as Reid won't allow him to walk behind, so just don't hit the old guy, just hit Reid" Russell instructed, both men whispering as only a thin door now separated them from Reid.

They could hear Reid and Pengilly talking from the landing and Russell and Chambers both knew that they were only seconds away from Reid walking through the door.

The judge had managed to urinate after what seemed like ages to Reid, he flushed the chain and had now turned to the sink to wash his hands, he was about to turn on the hot tap when he was grabbed by the arm and dragged out of the toilet by Reid, this happened to the annoyance of Pengilly "oh my lord, you have to let me wash my hands, it's disgusting" said Pengilly demandingly.

Reid closed the toilet door and with a few gentle pushes he then ushered the judge back down the hallway "you don't need to wash them judge, you're not baking a cake" he replied.

Chambers and Russell had now heard the toilet chain flush and could hear the voices getting louder so knew that they had only moments until the door was opened, Russell looked over at Chambers who was visibly shaking, he caught his eye and mouthed the words “are you ready?” to Chambers who just nodded back at him, Russell took a large intake of breath and waited.

Slowly the door to the cellar opened and Pengilly wandered through not knowing or expecting to see anyone at the top of the stairs, closely followed by Reid who again wasn’t expecting his two captives to be free, as the judge left the hall way and took his first steps onto the stairway landing leading to the cellar he caught sight of the two figures waiting for them at the doorway which startled him for a second and he gave out an involuntary yelp, this alerted Reid to the fact that something was wrong and within a fraction of a second later he suddenly saw the flash of chrome from the large shiny spanner coming quickly towards him, that was being wielded by Russell, as it came quickly crashing down towards his head, with cat like reactions Reid shoved Pengilly forwards sending him toppling down the stairs, this made Chambers lose his balance as the judge went hurtling past him.

Reid managed to twist his body, so the spanner struck him on the right shoulder so hard that he dropped the pistol, he winced with the pain that shot down his arm from the impact of the blow, and almost instantaneously Reid swung his large left fist which connected with forehead of Russell sending him falling backwards down the stairs following the judge all the way to the bottom, a different part of his body striking each hard wooden step as he fell.

Reid located the gun laying on the floor at the top of the stairs, but he never had time to retrieve it as he still had Chambers wielding a hammer, whom had now regained his balance.

He had raised it above his head and was ready to lower it at fast pace towards Reid, With his right shoulder in severe pain, he was used to ignoring and working through it, he flung himself forward towards Chambers so quickly that Chambers never had time to lower the hammer, grabbing hold of the arm holding the weapon, Chambers had hardly any strength and was no match for the muscular Reid, who disarmed him with a quick and skilful wrist lock, the hammer falling to the floor, he then made him join the other two with a quick shove causing him to fall backwards down the stairs until all three men were laid in a tangled heap at the bottom.

Reid quickly retrieved the pistol from the floor and with his right injured shoulder he raised it up and pointed it at the three men who all remained still and looked back up at Reid with worried expressions.

Reid stood for a while, his right shoulder throbbing after the strike with the spanner, he spent almost a minute attempting to work out how Chambers and Russell had freed themselves, the three men still tangled with each other at the foot of the stairs didn't dare move to sort themselves or get back to their feet, they just laid still with Russell and Chambers worried for their safety now their plan had gone wrong.

Pengilly was left stunned and angry that he had taken a fall because of their bungled escape attempt "you total and utter idiots" he shouted at the pair, Russell or Chambers never answered but just carried on looking at Reid.

Pengilly wanted to make an important point to Reid as he lay at the foot of the stairs in an entangled mess with the other two "I had nothing to do with this, if you think that this was somehow planned and my visit to the toilet was intended to distract you, then you're wrong, I had no idea these two fools where planning that" he pointed out to Reid forcefully.

Reid, from the top of the stairs and with the gun still pointing at the three, looked around the cellar and it wasn't long before he spotted the secateurs laying on the work bench right next to where Russell was sitting, next to them was the cut pieces of cable tie which once fastened both men to the table, Reid now had his answer to how they had escaped.

He looked down at the three hostages "I believe you judge; I know this was down to these two" he said to Pengilly's relief, Reid was injured and in pain from the strike but what bothered him more was that he felt disrespected by the escape attempt, he felt that Russell and Chambers obviously didn't fear him as much as he had thought.

If they did then they wouldn't have dared tried to escape or attack him like they just did, but what annoyed him even more than that was that he had gotten careless, he questioned himself in the moments he stood at the top of the stairway looking down at the three men, who were too scared to move with fear of being shot, maybe he was out of practice, or his mind wasn't fully switched on, maybe it was tiredness as he hadn't slept for over twenty-four hours.

But he knew for certain that he wouldn't make any more mistakes, he knew from experience that mistakes, in situations that he had been used to, get people hurt or killed, and he knew how important what he was doing was and he just could not afford to fail.

As he stared down at the three men, with shooting pains running down his right arm, he considered himself fortunate that he was able to correct the mistake he had made and that his plans where still very much intact.

CHAPTER FOURTEEN

The door to the command centre swung open and in stepped Karen, she looked around in order to find the person in charge when Tucker walked forward and introduced herself with her rank and name, she was then taken to the briefing area where she was introduced to Grey and the three of them sat at a table and discussed the situation.

Tucker was eager to move things on and now Karen had arrived they could finally open up some dialogue with Reid but first of all she wanted to know everything that Karen knew, after a few minutes Tucker had been made aware that Karen was the officer in charge of the case involving Reid's wife's death, and that Reid, in Karen's opinion, had been left devastated not just by her death but also by the outcome of the court case, Karen briefed Tucker on who Chambers was and also shone light on the fact that Bilton Russell was his barrister and that Pengilly was the judge who passed sentence.

Tucker now had a motive for why Reid had gone to such extremes as to take the three hostages, but she still didn't know why Reid was doing it or what he was hoping to achieve, that was something that she hoped would become clear whilst talking to Reid. First of all, Tucker wanted to make sure that Karen could and would say the correct things during the conversations with Reid.

"I'm sure you'll understand that because I don't know you Karen, that I'm unaware of any special skills that you may have" said Tucker in her soft tone, "for instance, are you a trained negotiator?" she asked, "No I'm not ma'am" replied Karen, who was instructed immediately by Tucker to call her by her first name instead of her rank or title.

Karen knew that it didn't matter what training she had or in this case didn't have, as it was Reid calling the shots and it was Reid who would insist that Karen be the one who would lead the telephone negotiations, although Tucker wasn't happy having to let an untrained negotiator do the negotiating she never had a choice and at least she would be by Karen's side to guide her along through the process.

"We have to play with the cards we're dealt and if Reid is insisting on having you as the lead then that's what we have to do" Tucker explained. However, there was a burning question that Tucker would hope Karen could put an answer too.

With Karen suddenly feeling like she was under interrogation, Tucker looked deep into her eyes and asked the question that was occupying her mind, she then wanted to watch Karen's response and her actions to see if she could pick anything up from it, she was fully aware that most of a person's communication comes from their body language and she was very good at reading it, she had outed many liars in the past with her skill in this area.

"I'm wondering why Steven Reid is so insistent on having you here, just how close did you two get to each other during the investigation of his wife's death?" Tucker asked, who had moved from friendly and informative to a more professional approach.

Karen's initial reaction was one of surprise, not by the question just asked to her but more because of the question or the type of question being asked so soon, herself and Reid knew that it would raise some suspicion as to why Reid wanted her there at all, never mind having her taking the lead, so they had several answers already prepared if and when such an issue was raised.

"with regards to closeness, myself and Steven were both left bitterly disappointed with the result of the court case" replied Karen confidently and she carried on her answer in the same manner.

"I think Steven has trust in me, so whatever it is he is wanting to get out of this, I think he wants to deal with a familiar and trusting person" Karen informed Tucker "I can't be certain, but if you wish, that can be one of the first things I'll ask" she replied, the words flowing from her lips in what she hoped wasn't to noticeable that they had been rehearsed.

Karen, wanted to avoid any kind of clash with Tucker so she was feeling somewhat disappointed with herself for giving such a sharp answer. She sat waiting for Tuckers response hoping that she hadn't just thrown down a gauntlet in any way.

Tucker took a breath and waited for a brief moment, giving her some time to get a feel of the atmosphere and to see if she could get anything from Karen's body language.

She looked directly at Karen and left just enough of a pause for her to see Karen getting a little uncomfortable, before she spoke "no need to ask him that Karen" Tucker replied, relieving Karen's tension "I was just curious that's all, we're lucky that he has trust in you as it will help our cause" said Tucker as she rose from her chair, and with an air of the dramatic, she ran her fingers through her thick blonde hair and took a look at her team "it's Showtime, let's get to work" she announced.

Tucker went on to give Karen a crash course on the do's and don'ts of hostage negotiations, keeping things basic as not to confuse her, Tucker would be at her side if anything came up that she couldn't handle, Tucker had no idea that Karen and Reid where working together, and she wasn't even thinking along those lines but one thing had left Tucker a little puzzled, one thing that she knew that no one else had picked up on, but she had, after only speaking with Karen for a few minutes, she wondered why Karen wasn't showing any nerves, here she is thrown into the deep end and with no negotiating training whatsoever coupled with the fact that the lives of three men were resting on her, and she was calm and in complete control of herself.

This issue would not be shared with anyone; she decided not to raise it just yet, neither with Karen or any of her trusted officers. She did however feel that this little thing that she had pinpointed was significant enough for her to have to monitor the situation covertly and she was perfectly placed to be able watch and listen as things moved forward.

The time had come that Tucker had been waiting for, now finally, after waiting for such a long time, they were about to open up negotiations with Reid, and even though Tucker had been relegated to what she saw as the subs bench, she was still in the position to control things and this was one of her areas of expertise and she had been itching to get working on it.

CHAPTER FIFTEEN

All three men where retied to the table using the same method as before. And they all sat in total silence, the cutters had been removed and where now safely stored in the tool box they had come from.

The atmosphere in the cellar at that time had become heavy and negative. Reid was pacing the floor, he was angry but was trying to not let his anger cloud his judgment, he rubbed his injured shoulder as he walked quickly around the wine racks muttering to himself.

"sloppy, I got sloppy" he said within ear shot of the others "I suppose I could put it down to tiredness, I haven't slept properly in days, but that simple mistake could have cost me" he said as if giving himself a telling off, He could feel his anger beginning to rise from the pit of his stomach, he questioned how Russell and Chambers could have even attempted such a daring escape, going round and round inside his head he played out a different scenario where they had been successful.

Reid had come through the door, only this time Russell had struck him with the giant spanner over the head before he could even react, in this version of events Russell showed his heroics by knocking Reid unconscious, as he laid motionless, the pool of blood that his limp body lay in becoming bigger by the second from the large wound to his skull, Russell lead Chambers and Pengilly to freedom and Reid woke up in hospital hours later, his skull fractured and he was under armed police guard, This is how it could have been, he thought to himself, and this was enough for him to stay alert and not make any more stupid mistakes.

As Reid walked aimlessly amongst the wine racks he was now being watched closely by Russell, to him Reid looked like he was unstable, as if the pressures of what he was doing had suddenly hit home.

He watched as Reid wandered around and around, muttering to himself as he did so, and suddenly, at that moment, Russell felt no fear of Reid, the man he was looking at just then, looked a little pathetic, as if desperately trying to find a solution to the situation he had got himself into, a man who was letting control slip through his fingers.

Russell watched Reid for a few more seconds and as those seconds passed Reid began to look more and more weak to Russell, while Russell himself began to feel more confident, even though he was injured from the escape attempt and he was tied to the table again, Russell had convinced himself that he could defeat Reid with mind games and break him down over time with the power of words, which he had made a living from.

He then noticed Reid hold onto his injured shoulder with his left arm, he witnessed as Reid moved the injured arm slowly in a circular motion to stop his heavily bruised and possibly fractured shoulder from seizing up. The grimace on Reid's face brought some satisfaction to Russell "how's your shoulder?" he said in a sarcastic tone.

Reid stopped dead on the spot and took a quick glimpse over to Russell who was smiling back at him out of total disrespect, Reid had to act, he could not let Russell get away with such a remark and he had to regain the fear factor that he believed he once held.

Reid had an instant idea “well let’s see shall we” Reid replied, with speed and power Reid pushed the wine rack closest to him over, it hit the rack next to it and like dominoes they both were sent crashing to the floor, the loud bang they made as their heavy wooden frames smashed onto the concrete made Pengilly and Chambers jump with shock.

Russell saw as dozens of his precious wine bottles shattered upon impact with the cellar floor, Reid carried on, one by one he pulled or pushed over the remaining wine racks, each one making the same or sometimes louder noise as the sound amplified around the cold cellar.

Russell begged Reid to stop “please, stop this, I am truly sorry for what I did, please don’t destroy my collection” he pleaded with Reid in a panic, but his words where ignored.

With the three hostages looking on Reid wandered around the rubble of broken glass bottles and puddles of expensive wine as the concrete floor began to soak it up, he searched for the bottles which hadn't been broken on impact.

With each bottle he found that was still intact and had survived the fall, Reid chose a wall to throw it against, with each throw he shouted loudly "my shoulder seems fine" or "no problem with that throw" and "just a little stiff, but its working okay" he bellowed, taunting Russell who was now shaking his head in disbelief and who was now the one feeling weak and pathetic.

shards of broken glass and sprays of extremely expensive red and white wine flew across the room, covering the three men who were attempting to duck down into their seats trying not to be hit by any of the flying debris.

Reid carried on searching the floor for unbroken bottles, kicking away the piles of broken glass in order to locate any full ones, any he found where thrown powerfully against a different wall each time.

the three men tightly closed their eyes to protect them from the small fragments of glass that were sent spinning in the air on impact. Almost every surface had puddles of wine dripping of it, the walls of the cellar stained with wine, some of the walls had wine running down them, and the ceiling dripped wine over the three men.

Russell felt like his heart had been torn from his body and he experienced the dreadful feeling as his soul sank into the depths of despair, dragging him down with it as he watched the collection he had dedicated decades too being destroyed mercilessly by Reid.

He watched with tears in his eyes as the most important thing he had in his life, the thing he cherished more than even his own wife was crushed and smashed to pieces in front of him and there was nothing he could do to stop it.

He looked on helplessly as his entire collection become shattered to smithereens and left into fragments on the floor by this stranger who had invaded his life, a very valuable collection that he had spent years upon years, searching for and building was destroyed in under three minutes by Reid who lapped up the feeling of satisfaction and thrived on the enjoyment and exhilaration as he ripped apart Russell's most precious possession.

Reid had kept the last two bottles that had not been broken, he made a good search of the floor to make sure that these where the last two remaining bottles of what was once an impressive collection, he took hold of one bottle in each hand, he walked over to Russell and stood directly in front of him "it seems my shoulder is fine" he said in his gruff cold tone, panting moderately after the high intensity workout.

Without blinking he raised both his arms from his side to shoulder height and then brought them down together at speed, both the bottles connected and smashed into dozens of pieces, the wine from both bottles splashed over all four men and Reid was left with just the jagged razor-sharp neck of both bottles in his hands, he tossed them both over his shoulder, walked to his chair and tipped it forward so to wipe the quantity of wine that covered the seat and sat down facing the three.

Russell was sickened by what he had witnessed, he looked around the cellar at the aftermath of the destruction of his valuable hobby that he was so passionate about and proud of, with tears clearly visible in his eyes he shook his head "You are scum, that is all you are and you're going to rot in prison, I'll see that you do" Russell spat the words out with frustration and anger.

Reid, while sitting, moved some of the broken glass towards the wall with his feet "think of it this way Oliver, after your escape attempt I could have destroyed your wine or destroy you, you're lucky I chose the wine" Reid replied.

Reid no longer felt the anger burning inside of him and he felt that the destruction of the hundreds of bottles and the financial loss of Russell's collection was punishment enough for the escape attempt and for the injury that he now had.

Chambers, as usual was sitting quietly avoiding any eye contact with Reid, Russell was visibly upset and Pengilly was wearing an expression of disgust, Reid noticed this and wanted to find out why "what's on your mind judge?" he asked Pengilly took a few moments to think about his reply "you have just shown yourself for what you really are" he replied, Reid sat forward in his seat intrigued, and with a look of expectancy on his face he replied "what is that judge? I'd like to know what it is you think I am" he asked, Before Pengilly could

answer and to the disappointment of Reid, their conversation was interrupted by the mobile phone, it had been silent for over an hour and the sudden loud ringing filled the air of the cellar, Reid hoped that this would be the call he was waiting for, if it was he wouldn't be to annoyed about the interruption.

All three hostages looked at Reid expectantly as the sound of the phone echoed around the cellar, the ringing sound seemed to be bouncing off the walls. Reid calmly walked over to it as it laid on the table and glanced down at the screen.

He looked up at the three men and smiled, Reid then picked up the ringing phone and with it resting in the palm of his hand he took a calming breath, letting it out slowly "it looks like this could be it boys" he said, his face serious he readied himself for what would be the most important phone call of his life.

CHAPTER SIXTEEN

Tucker, Grey and Karen where sat around the table, in the background was a splattering of officers all manning their posts and who would be carrying out their roles as the negotiations went on. Standing in the middle of the table was the telephone that Tucker hoped would be the valuable tool that would bring an end to this siege.

They had the phone on loud speaker and sat waiting as the phone rang, waiting for Reid to answer it, they didn't have to wait very long. "Who am I speaking to?" was Reid's response, as he answered the ringing phone.

His voice sounded loud and clear through the speaker. Tucker took the lead at this point "good afternoon Steven, its Jo

Tucker, you'll be pleased to know that I'm sitting here with Karen Caswell" she replied.

Tucker was one of the most experienced officers on the force, and she was clever, she was prepared to play whatever game Reid was planning and she was also prepared to use Karen as spokesperson under her guidance, she never lost sight of the main agenda which was Reid was an armed and dangerous man, He was an ex-soldier so knew how to handle weapons and had the mind-set that would enable him to pull the trigger if he needed to, Tucker was also very much aware that Reid doesn't mind inflicting pain on others, he showed that with the three men in the pub car park, so Tucker knew the kind of man she was dealing with, she now needed to know the reason behind the armed siege.

Karen had been briefed well by Tucker, one of the things she stressed was to try and accommodate anything that Reid asks for, as long as it's realistic, Tucker said it was important to lead Reid down a certain road and if it took being a yes man to get him there then Tucker was more than willing to do it "You have to kiss arse, before you can kick arse" Tucker said, that phrase took a little bit of thinking time for Karen but once she had worked it out its meaning was absolutely correct.

With the phone lines now live and active the negotiations would now take place and Tucker and her team would find out what Reid was wanting out of this whole thing. Tucker gave Karen, the nod to begin and she opened up with a basic introduction and question "hi Steven its Karen, how are you?" she asked in a sheepish manner. "I'm good thanks Karen, glad you could make it" he replied politely, he paused waiting for Karen to speak as he did he got himself into a comfortable position by leaning the chair onto its rear legs, the two front legs hovering off the wine stained concrete floor and resting both his feet up against the workbench, this gave the impression to the three watching hostages that he was preparing for a long conversation.

He coolly placed both his hands behind his head and with the phone resting up against the vice and on loud speaker he could talk freely, and everyone could hear. Karen cleared her throat and attempted to appear a little more confident "so Steven, what's all this about" she asked, looking at Tucker for approval.

Again, Reid's reply was straight to the point and quick "it's about getting to the truth" he said, then there was more silence as he waited for a reply, Karen looked across the table to where Tucker was sitting for some guidance, Tucker took this as her cue to step in for a brief moment "Steven, its Jo Tucker, before you say anything, I know you want to deal with Karen but I'm wondering why that is, no offence to her but she isn't trained in this sort of thing and I think it would be better if you let me have a more active role in these negotiations" she said, looking over at Karen as she spoke and mouthing the "that's fair enough", Karen nodded in reply.

There was a brief silence as the three police officers sat around the table and looked at each other, just when Tucker was beginning to wonder if Reid was going to reply he did so "I trust Karen, and I want her to do the talking because she will be sincere and not speak to me in a trained methodical way" he replied, even before Tucker could give any response Reid piped up again "please be aware officer Tucker that there are going to be no negotiations here today, there is nothing to negotiate, I'm simply going to make sure that we all hear the truth then you can come in and make the relevant arrests, do you understand?" said Reid in a forthright way.

It wasn't tucker who answered, it was Karen who took the lead "you say you want the truth, but that is what you got in court Steven, you may not have agreed with it, but it is the law of the land and we must abide by it" she said, which prompted a nod of satisfaction from Tucker, Reid replied with conviction "the so called truth that was told in court was orchestrated, a practiced story, a lie made up by a clever barrister, his client and a crooked judge, I'm going to get to the truth, the real truth, under my terms and my conditions" Reid said those words with his eyes fixed permanently on his captives, Pengilly shaking his head in disagreement.

"So how do you intend to get to this truth?" asked Karen, "by using the only method I know how, and which has worked well many times, before" was Reid's reply, Karen looked over at Tucker who gave her a nod to go ahead and ask the next obvious question, “and this method is?” Karen said with her gaze firmly fixed on Tucker while waiting for the answer.

Ten long seconds passed without a word from Reid, Karen was looking at Tucker, Tucker looking at the phone along with Grey and still no reply came, eventually, when Tucker could take no more of the awkward silence she spoke “I know you’re still there Steven, and we would like an answer please” she asked another few seconds passed, Reid enjoyed the long silences and used them to good effect, which infuriated Tucker, while Tucker fixed her gaze directly at the phone she was unaware that down in the cellar Reid was calmly looking around the cellar still in his relaxed seated position, purposely pausing for thought for as long as he felt necessary.

Eventually, after half a minute of nothing but silence Reid decide to answer “when soldiers are dropped over enemy lines, and can sometimes end up captured, nasty things can happen, not to me but a few friends of mine" he said, his voice seemed to be louder and it rang around the command centre for all to hear clearly, he carried on with the full attention of everyone listening, "when you end up being questioned by the enemy it isn't nice, and they use methods which are deemed to be barbaric, but the politicians don't tell the public that part" Reid rose from his chair and grabbed the phone, holding it like a walkie talkie he approached Chambers and looked down at him as he spoke, Chambers avoided eye contact and remained with his head down, as Reid carried on "sometimes it can be sadistic, even medieval, that's why a certain type of soldier is used in operations where capture is a possibility" he said with his eyes burning into the top of Chambers' head, Chambers could feel Reid staring at him, he could feel the tension in the room, and the sound of Reid's voice was making him all the more nervous as Reid carried on talking into the phone having gained the full attention of every officer listening "that type of soldier is highly trained to withstand these methods, to block out the pain and to have the strength of mind not to break" Reid's voice now sounding more sadistic with every sentence.

At this point Tuckers expression was one of concern while she listened in on what Reid was saying "I know this for certain, there is only one man in this room who has that kind of training, and it's not any of the three men I'm looking at right now" when Reid had finished talking, he slowly lowered the phone away from his mouth as he maintained his glare at the top of Chambers' head.

Chambers wanted to look up at Reid, but he was to scared, he was literally forcing himself to remain looking down at the table, like a small child seeking safety, his shoulders hunched, and head tucked into his chest, but he could feel Reid's presence and his stare felt like it was drilling into him.

Tucker stood up quickly from her seat, she knew, as did everyone else, exactly what Reid was referring to and she could not stand by and say nothing "Steven, judging by what you have just said, I take it that you intend to torture those people?" she asked worryingly.

It was at this point that Chambers could not hold his position anymore and he raised his head slowly when he heard what Tucker had just asked, for the first time he looked at Reid, who was standing just inches away from him, directly in the eyes, his expression was one of pure fear, he carried on looking at Reid as Reid glared back at him, because of the withdrawal from drugs and the state of fear his mind was in he began to hallucinate, as he looked at Reid, his entire eye balls seemed to be black in colour, he got the sense that Reid was without a soul, like he was empty inside and the only thing on his mind was to hurt him, his heightened mixed up senses made it feel like he was facing the devil in the face and he has never felt fear like it before.

Tucker tried to reason with Reid “Steven, there are better ways to do this, you are not in a war zone now, those men are not enemy soldiers” she said hurriedly “no, but they are my enemy” he replied, Karen this time was the one who spoke “Steven, stop this before you even start it, and I promise we will do another thorough investigation into what happened the night your wife was killed” she pleaded “but do not torture those men, you are making it worse for yourself” she explained, Tucker was now on red alert, she could not allow Reid to carry out his threat, She quickly leant over and pressed mute on the phone and told Grey to get Danks from the armed response team, as Grey left he could hear Reid’s reply to Karen’s statement “there is no further investigations necessary, this is the only way” was Reid’s reply.

Tucker, who now felt a sense of urgency and was feeling like she had been backed into a corner and forced to act spoke again "Steven, listen to me, we cannot stand by while you torture those men, if you do then I will have no option other than to send in my team of armed officers, now as a former soldier you know that is not what you want to happen, this can be resolved peacefully" she said in an ordering tone, Reid's voice remained calm and answered her in the same sinister tone, "I wouldn't do that if I were you Tucker, my particular role in the army was as an explosives expert, and this entire house is rigged to blow when I press the button on the remote control I'm holding, so unless you want the deaths of the hostages, myself and your armed response team on your conscience, I'd hold them back" he said, he paused for a few seconds, making sure that he had Tuckers attention before he carried on."if I so much as hear a single officer trying to gain entry to this house, then please believe me, I will blow this entire place to pieces, the blast radius of which would wipe out half of this area" Reid again paused for effect.

This stopped Tucker in her tracks, she knew that she could not call Reid's bluff in case he had wired the house with explosives, and what she needed now was her negotiation skills. Karen had taken one look at Tuckers reaction to this information and knew that it had, had an impact and she wanted to feed Reid this information, "Steven, why don't we all take a little while to collect our thought? I'm sure you could do with a drink I know my mouth feels like the Sahara Desert" Karen said.

Steven immediately recognised the safe word and knew that Karen wanted to talk to him urgently, so he acted according to the plan and made an excuse to halt the phone call.

With Tuckers mind now working overtime trying to figure out what to do, all she could come up with was to try and stall Reid with his actions, Reid was still standing staring down at Chambers who was frozen with fear, he took the opportunity to put a halt to the call and then wait for Karen to ring him with whatever information she had for him.

"I'm going to hang up for a few minutes, I have a few things to prepare, so ring me back in twenty minutes" announced Reid, Tucker looked panicked "what do you need to prepare Steven?" she asked, Reid didn't explain but just simply replied "ring back in twenty" he then gave a big sinister grin directed towards Chambers who screamed for help just a second Reid hung up the phone.

Tucker and the others where left stunned, they all heard Chambers scream out in fear for his safety just as the line went dead, but this was nothing that Tucker or the rest had experienced before, and she was searching for an answer, She looked sternly at Karen "why did you call a halt?" she asked in a sharp tone of voice, Karen acted flustered "I'm sorry, I just thought it would buy us a bit of time, and it did" she replied, Grey who was standing next to Tucker agreed with Karen "she got us twenty minutes Jo" he said, and tucker was forced to agree.

It was that moment Danks burst into the command room, he approached Tucker and she quickly briefed him on the situation, for the first time in her long career Tucker was struggling for ideas and she was beginning to feel the pressure.

She couldn't find an answer to the problem that Reid had set, if the house was rigged to blow then there was little chance of anyone being able to gain entry to the house and taking Reid down, but she also knew that she could not sit back and listen to Reid torture the hostages and do nothing.

Tuckers mind was going in several different directions at once and the lives of three men where resting on whatever decision she made, one thing that Tucker kept thinking, and hoping she was correct in thinking it, was that Reid was bluffing and there were no explosives, but how would she find that out, she would have to know all about Reid's army background and if he could make explosives, if so could he get hold of the materials necessary.

Tucker certainly believed that Reid was the kind of man who would use the explosives if he had them and he felt that he needed too, and she needed a solution and one that would make sure that none of the hostages were harmed or killed.

CHAPTER SEVENTEEN

The scene was now set as far as Reid was concerned, while he waited for Karen to call, he had released Chambers from his ties and forcefully dragged him the short distance across to the workbench and with one arm cable tied to the leg of the heavy workbench, he had placed his right arm into the vice and fastened it tightly enough so that he couldn't release it.

Although Chambers was a very skinny man because of the drugs he had pumped into his frail looking body, the vice was gripping him so tightly that what little flesh his arms had was protruding out of the jaws of the vice and he had trouble moving his fingers or making a fist.

By now Chambers was a wreck, the tears were rolling down his face and he was so frightened that his begging for mercy was sometimes inaudible through the crying, wailing and hyperventilating, Pengilly and Russell looked on, both feeling helpless as they watched Reid cold heartedly ignore Chambers' pleas, his main concern was waiting for the phone to ring, so he could speak to Karen in private.

Outside in the command centre, Tucker was trying to figure out the best way to handle this situation, the head of the armed response was eager to send in his best team, but she was cautious of the threat of explosives, just to be certain that it was no idle threat she had confirmed with Karen that Reid was indeed an explosives expert in the army and this made her all the more cautious.

The decision was on tucker to lead her team in the correct way, she knew that she could not sit back and allow Reid to torture the hostages but she also knew that it was a massive risk to send in a hit team when the pressing of a single button would blow up the house and put more lives at risk, and she knew deep in her heart that Reid was definitely the kind of man who, if he needed to, would press the button and kill anyone close to the blast.

Karen made her excuses and said she had to check in at home before leaving the command centre, leaving Tucker and the rest of the team with the dilemma of working out how best to handle the situation. Karen left the command centre and she walked towards the edge of the cordon with her phone in her hand and was certain that no one was around, and she could talk in private.

Reid was standing holding his phone and watching Chambers fall apart right before his eyes when the phone started to ring, he looked at the screen and saw that it was Karen, so he walked to the other end of the cellar amongst the broken wine bottles that lay strewn around before he answered it, "what's the problem?" Reid asked, "there isn't one" Karen replied, "it's just an update" she informed Reid.

Reid listened closely to Karen and spoke in hushed tones, so the three men couldn't hear "you have them all in a panic, up until you mentioned the explosives I was certain that they were going to storm the house but now Tucker doesn't know what to do" she said.

Since Reid was over the other side of the cellar Pengilly was trying to reassure Chambers that things would be ok, deep down he had no idea if they actually where going to be, but he had to try something, Chambers was such a nervous wreck the words of Pengilly didn't make much sense to him.

Chambers had tried a few times to pull his arm out of the vice, but it was so tightly fastened, and he was so weak, it just never budged and with his left arm fastened to the table leg he felt helpless.

Russell however wasn't taking much notice of Chambers' plight, his interest was caught by Reid's telephone conversation, he was an intelligent man with a quick thinking brain and he had worked out that any previous phone conversations where done on loud speaker for everyone to hear but this one was being held in private, he turned to Pengilly and pointed this out "who do you think he's talking too?" he asked, Pengilly was too concerned for the welfare of Chambers "what does it matter, I'm more worried about this young chap" he replied.

Russell at this point couldn't take his eyes off Reid, and he became more suspicious by the second "don't you think it's weird how he doesn't want us to hear what he's saying or for us to know who he is talking to?" asked Russell in a whisper, but again, Pengilly wasn't paying full attention to what Russell was attempting to point out as his only concern was for Chambers.

Russell's full attention was on Reid, he watched him as he stood side on to him and he seemed to be having an in-depth discussion with someone, his demeanour didn't seem uneasy or in any way worried.

Russell came to the conclusion that whatever was being said, it was being said by someone on his side, someone who was helping Reid as judging by his reactions to the person on the other end of the phone it looked like he was being fed information that was aiding him, Russell turned to Pengilly again "he is being helped, he has someone on the inside" he stated, this time Pengilly took notice "what on earth makes you say that?" he asked, Russell quickly explained to the judge his theory and it seemed so concrete that even Pengilly had to agree that it was a possibility.

But even though they were armed with this information Russell and Pengilly both knew that there was little they could do with it and it was Pengilly who pointed that out to a disappointed Russell.

Reid informed Karen that he had moved Chambers over to the vice, but Karen showed some concern with what Reid had instore for chambers "don't go overboard Steven, just enough to get him to talk ok" she said, Reid felt a little offended by the remark as he had been doing this form of interrogation longer than Karen had been walking but he humoured her with his reply "yeah, just enough Karen" he replied.

They ended the phone call with them both feeling like they had full control of the situation and all they had to do was stick to the plan and keep their wits about them, before they hung up the phone Karen informed Reid of the new safe word "Niagara Falls, if you hear that, you know what to do" she said, Reid acknowledged it and Karen knew that Reid was a professional and that he could be relied on, they ended the call and both went back to their business.

CHAPTER EIGHTEEN

Tucker was clock watching, there was three minutes left until they rang Reid back and she was playing it by the rules, she was following Reid's instructions to the letter.

Karen had re-joined the team after her secret phone call to Reid, and it seemed to her that Tucker and the team had no plan in place on how to counter act Reid's intentions.

Tucker had a worried look on her face, she knew that after all her successes over the decades, if she had a bad result here then that is what she would be remembered for, but worse than that she had the lives of three men resting on every decision that she made, and she was starting to feel the pressure bearing down on her.

While Karen was out of the room, Tucker had asked sergeant Danks to join her in the command centre, with minutes to go until the call had to be made Tucker took Danks into a corner of the room for a little chat, this alerted Karen as she couldn't hear what was being said, she was sitting over the other side of the command centre and all she could see was Tucker and Danks stood in close proximity to each other talking quietly and for some reason no one other than Tucker and Danks was a part of it.

Very quietly she engaged Danks in conversation "do you think you could get a team inside the house without Reid knowing they were there?" she asked, with a smile Danks nodded "absolutely, I could have four of my best men positioned outside that cellar door waiting to burst in on my order, and that prick wouldn't have a clue" was his reply.

Tucker had realised over the break in negotiations, that Reid said he had a remote control to detonate the explosives, which meant that the house was not booby trapped and rigged to blow when someone entered, she took advantage of Reid's slip of the tongue and knew that this was her best and only chance to get some men on the inside, but wanted to keep this information down to a selected few people, strictly on a need to know basis.

Tucker thought for a brief second about Danks' answer, she fully aware that she was low on options and that this idea was probably her best, and Danks agreed with her, she instructed Danks to get his team together and remain on standby until she gave the order, she wanted first to see if she could still handle things with negotiations rather than force.

As Danks hurriedly left the command centre he was watched by Karen who was concerned to know what had just gone on, and was eager to find out from Tucker.

She strolled over to her when Tucker had returned to the table and began dialling Reid's number "are you using the response team?" Karen politely asked, while Tucker sat and waited for the call to connect, she looked up at Karen "it's an option, one I'd rather not use but one I may have to" she replied.

This wasn't the answer that Karen wanted to hear, she needed to alert Reid of the possible intervention, but couldn't make another excuse to leave the command centre so soon after just returning, so for now she would have to monitor the situation.

As Reid's phone rang in the cellar he prepared himself for what was to come, he let the phone ring a few times which worried Tucker since any other call had been answered within two rings, Reid seemed to be playing and winning the mind games, he took a few deep breaths for composure as the ringing of the phone sounded around the cellar, six rings, turned to seven which turned to eight, Tucker looked at Karen as if searching for an answer to why Reid was not answering, but Karen just looked back at her dumbfounded.

Pengilly and Russell were both sat staring at Reid as the phone kept ringing, the sound of which reverberated around the open space in which they were sitting, Russell, in his mind, was willing Reid to answer it.

Ten rings had now been and gone, then eleven, then twelve, Reid took a few more breaths until he was certain that his mind set was focussed totally on the job, he took one last look at chambers who was sitting forward in his seat with his arm looking more and more uncomfortable locked in the vice, his body language spoke of a man that was already broken, and very frightened at what was going to happen to him.

The ringing phone had now hit fifteen rings as Reid slowly reached down and picked it up off the table, sixteen then seventeen rings went by as he calmly pressed the answer key and simply said "hello" to the relief of Tucker, "I was beginning to think you were ignoring me" she said before any other words could be said by either person, Russell, who had been planning this since he saw Reid talking on the phone to a mystery person, began shouting at the top of his voice so Tucker could clearly hear him, "he's working with someone on the inside" he shouted out to the surprise of everyone, this outburst stunned Reid as he was unsure of what Russell was doing, but Russell carried on "he's talking to someone on your end, you have a spy in your camp" Russell shouted as loudly as he could, to make sure that the person on the other end of the phone would hear.

Tucker was also taken aback "who is that shouting?" she asked, Reid never got chance to answer as Russell shouted out again "he is getting inside help" he screamed, suddenly Reid realised what Russell was referring to and cut off Tucker by hanging up the phone.

Reid looked over at Russell in astonishment, but fury soon replaced this emotion and in one fluid motion he walked the five or six steps up to Russell and hit him across the face with the hand that was clutching the phone, the pain Russell felt was immense as the stinging feeling caused by the strike lingered and he closed his eyes as he winced, but he was proud of himself for what he had done and hoped that it had thrown a spanner into the works of Reid's plan.

Pengilly on the other hand couldn't understand why Russell would put himself in harm's way the way he just had and wasn't wholly sure what he hoped to achieve by his outburst.

Within the command centre Tucker was left speechless for a few moments, she looked at Grey "what the hell was that about?" she asked, Grey who looked just as bemused replied "did he say, he has inside help?" Tucker looked over at Karen who was holding her nerve very well "yes he did" replied Tucker to Greys question, while staring over at Karen.

Karen, with her poker face well and truly on joined in the discussion, "have you any idea who that was shouting?" she asked playing the role of concerned police officer "or who is supposed to be the inside man?" she asked with concern.

Tuckers quick thinking brain was firing rapidly, she had her suspicions but didn't want to play her hand until she was certain, so she decided to play her cards close to her chest "let's get him back on the phone and see if we can find out" she said without giving anything away.

Reid, was something of a control freak, he had a solid plan that he was following, and he didn't like it at all when people got in the way and put that plan in jeopardy and it had happened several times from the moment he had taken on this venture, but he was professional enough and smart enough to think on his feet and deal with the situation.

What Russell had done here though, Reid didn't see as a hindrance, he knew it wouldn't alter the plan, however he was now concerned for Karen, but he knew that she could take care of herself, so whatever was happening at the other end, he could not let it affect what he was doing.

The phone rang as Reid had expected it to, before he answered it however he picked up the pistol which had been laid redundant for a while on the work bench and pressed it up against the forehead of Russell "you utter one more word, and ill blow your brains out through the back of your skull" he said with a venomous tone to his voice.

Russell, who hoped his actions had harmed Reid's plan in some way, never replied or reacted to the threat, he just sat feeling the cold steel of the gun barrel on his skin and looked back at

Reid, he was scared, as he had been many times during this ordeal, but he was learning how to suppress it.

Reid answered the phone with a sharp “hello” he knew that Tucker was going to want to know some details of what just happened, but he wasn’t prepared to give anything away.

“Hello Steven, Jo Tucker here” she said quickly “who was that shouting in the back ground?” Tucker asked immediately, Reid answered flippantly in an attempt to get passed it “just one of my over confident house guests, it won’t happen again” he replied. Tucker’s main concern was for the safety of the hostages and with the last remark that Reid had just made she was concerned for the health of whoever it was who shouted out “I hope you haven’t hurt that person Steven” she stated, Reid was eager to regain control of the situation and he felt that the best way to do this was not to dwell on what Russell had done, “no one has been hurt” he informed Tucker “let’s get back to business, and you can start by telling me why I’m talking to you and not Karen?” Reid asked in a demanding tone.

his thinking with that question was twofold, one, he could check on Karen’s welfare to see if the police had taken Russell’s statement seriously and if she was under any suspicion and two, he could get things back on track and let the police believe that all is well, and that Karen is not the so called inside man.

Tucker’s response was not what Reid was expecting, “Karen is here, but I’m going to be doing a lot of the talking, as it seems to me that you’re willing to take this to the extremes and I wouldn’t be able to live with myself if I didn’t at least try to talk you out of it” she said with an air of authority clearly heard in her forthright tone, Reid thought about this for a second, he never really needed Karen to take the lead in the negotiations, the whole point of insisting on that, was just to make sure that Karen was always present, so she could secretly relay any important information to him throughout the siege, But even though Tucker was now retaking the lead role, Karen would still be present, he came to the conclusion that it may work in their benefit if Karen faded into the background a little bit, so he nonchalantly agreed with Tuckers decision and carried on by describing the scene inside the cellar.

Reid's voice echoed around the cellar as he spoke "This is how things are right now" he said, "I have moved Chambers, the weakest of the three, over to the work bench where his left arm is securely tied to the leg of the bench and his right arm is currently jammed into a vice" explained Reid.

Tucker listened carefully, she knew that things where now getting very serious, and as she listened to what else Reid had to say, she was contemplating in her mind about using the tactical armed response team.

Reid, who was never much of a conversationalist, kept his description of what was about to happen very basic and brief, this was the part of the siege where he and the police would hear the truth.

“I want you and the rest of your team to listen to what Chambers has to say” explained Reid “I’m going to get the truth out of him, because if I’m not satisfied with any of the answers I’m given then ill tighten the vice” Reid explained to the listening police, “judging by his skinny arms, I don’t think it’ll take long before his radius bone snaps” he said, leaving some people listening at a loss due to the medical terminology.

Tucker, whilst listening to Reid, picked up on the fact that a few people didn't know what the radius bone was, Karen being one of them, so she pointed to her own forearm to indicate where the bone is situated. Reid was eager to get things started, so he placed his phone on the table near to where chambers was sitting, checked to make sure that Tucker and the others could hear him clearly, to which Tucker confirmed that they could.

Before Tucker could speak, Reid also wanted to know that they could hear when Chambers spoke, he grabbed hold of Chambers face with his left hand and glared into his eyes "say your name" he said "Craig Chambers" he replied, stuttering and with a very shaky voice, and his whole body trembling with fear "did you all hear that ok?" enquired Reid, Tucker needed to speak to Reid in the hope that she could talk him out of what he was about to do, so she used the opportunity of confirming that she heard Chambers clearly as her chance to hopefully get through to him.

“Steven, I’m asking you now, I’m pleading with you, don’t do what you’re about to do” said Tucker, as she looked out of the window at the heavily armed team of four men standing in a group talking, just waiting for the order to go in.

Reid wasn’t in the mood for debating with Tucker and simply repeated the question “tell me if you heard Chambers clearly?” he said bluntly, saddened by Reid’s lack of cooperation Tucker knocked on the window, gently but loud enough for Danks to hear and turn around and face her “we heard him Steven” she replied in a sad tone, then she nodded her head to Danks to send in his men, “but you are making a big mistake” Tucker continued to say.

She felt uneasy having to send in the troops, but she was also not happy about having to listen to a man being tortured and she could not stand by and let it happen, so her hand was forced, and she had no other option but to act.

Danks assembled his men, he was eager for his men to impress, he had been a part of so many sieges like this in the past but rarely does he or his men get the opportunity to flex their muscles and engage the enemy.

He seemed to thrive on the challenge and he knew only too well just how good his team was after being trained by him personally. Once in the house, Danks was confident that Reid would be taken down and the hostages would be unharmed, and this was the only way it was going to happen as he felt the time for any successful negotiations had been and gone.

CHAPTER NINETEEN

Tucker watched from the window of the command centre as the four heavily armed officers, wearing black boiler suits, bullet proof vests and helmets with blacked out visors ran towards the house in formation, each man was armed with Heckler and Koch semi-automatic rifles and carried Glock pistols in their holsters, as well as stun and smoke grenades about their person.

Sergeant Danks had taken up a position inside the centre alongside Tucker, Grey and Karen and was in constant communication with his four officers via radio which they wore as ear pieces, leaving their hands free to handle their weapons.

Any radio chatter had to be kept to a minimum as Tucker had Reid on the telephone and they didn't want him hearing any radio dialogue between Danks and his team that might alert him to the fact that they were moving in.

The plan was simplistic but relied on precise timing, the four officers had to break into the house as quietly as they could without alerting Reid, then once in they had to position themselves outside the cellar door and wait silently there for the order to move in, They had no idea how long they might be waiting, it could be minutes or hours but once the order was given, one of the officers would smash down the wooden cellar door using a large red metal door buster, known as the enforcer, which is a hand held battering ram, it is more ideally suited for smashing in thicker and more superior exterior doors with dead locks and bolts, So in comparison, a thin wooden interior door would be no challenge for which ever officer it was who would be wielding it, once the door was taken out the officers would have just seconds to rush into the cellar as quickly and swiftly as they could as the element of surprise would at this point be lost, between the four of them they would have to locate Reid and shoot him dead. before he could press the button on the remote control which would detonate the explosives he had rigged up and hidden around the house.

It was a plan that carried some risk but Danks was very confident that his highly trained men could carry it off successfully, although his men were also confident that it could be done in a matter of a few seconds, they were hoping that since Reid would not be aware of the officer's presence he wouldn't be anywhere near the remote when the officers burst in, giving them a few extra valuable seconds and also meaning that a kill shot might not be needed, and they could just wound Reid and apprehend him therefore bringing an end to the siege successfully.

Tuckers role was to keep Reid occupied so he would not be aware of the assault and hopefully be unprepared for it when it happened.

Every officer at the scene watched with their hearts in their mouths, as the four specialist officers approached the house, Karen was frantically trying to find a way of getting a message to Reid to warn him of the potential trouble heading his way, she had the safe word but now that Tucker was taking the lead in the talks with Reid it could be tricky to get the opportunity to use it. In the cellar and completely unaware of what was going on just outside the house, Reid placed a stool directly opposite Chambers and sat on it, he calmly placed one hand on the vice handle, Chambers looked directly at Reid with tear filled eyes, "please, please don't hurt me anymore" he said with a quiver to his voice that made him sound like a child in trouble as he begged for mercy.

In the command centre Tucker had one eye on the officers, who she could see from her window in the distance and had one ear on the radio listening to Danks and his men and the other ear on the telephone listening to Reid.

Reid gave a brief introduction before he started, “I don’t want to hurt you Craig, all you have to do is tell the truth” he said in reply to Chambers’ early plea not to hurt him.

The four officers had reached the door and after a quick investigation, they reported to Danks that it was too solid and would make too much noise to use that as a point of entry, instead they each made their way over to one of the windows to the right of the door, it was made up of thirty-six smaller square windows in a six by six formation, it had a simple sliding lock and it slid open with the bottom part of the window overlapping the top one, It was ideal and meant they were still in full view of Tucker and the rest. Back in the cellar, Reid spoke slowly so Chambers could understand through his crying and stressed state what was being said "tell me why you chose my wife's car to steal that night?" he asked very politely considering the circumstances, Chambers was shaking his head in a panic "it was just there, it was random honestly" he replied quickly, his words rushed and with genuine fear in his voice.

Reid didn't show any emotion but instead he turned the vice handle a couple of inches tightening the vice, Chambers' screams of pain could be heard by everyone, Tucker closed her eyes as she listened in on the phone, Russell and Pengilly, who were witnessing it, both looked away, and the four officers who were now making plans on how to gain entry through the window looked at each other in shock, as the screams where so loud they could be heard from outside the house.

Reid asked the same question again, and he received the same answer, as he turned the handle this time it made a creaking sound as it tightened around Chambers' arm, but this noise was drowned out by the loud shrieking screams coming from chambers as he felt the pressure of the vice tighten around his arm so much that it forced the blood down into his hand and pump to his fingertips, making it feel like they were about to burst open.

This time one of the officers used the screaming of chambers as sound cover to smash one of the smaller square windows and reached inside to undo the lock, it worked well as Reid never heard the breaking of the glass.

Tucker, whose heart was beating so fast that she could feel it against her chest wall, pleaded with Reid to stop "Steven, stop this, I cannot stand by while you torture a person" she shouted down the phone at Reid, “you have no choice inspector, but Chambers does, all he has to do is answer my questions” he replied, shouting over the noise of Chambers.

Karen was by now secretly frantic, she could see that officers where fiddling with the window lock and would soon be preparing to climb inside the house and she knew that Reid was unaware of this, but she couldn’t find a way of warning him, she repeatedly looked out of the window at the four marksmen and then back at the phone, her brain was searching for a way to get a warning to Reid, and all the time she had to look normal or as normal as a person can be when hearing someone being tortured.

Reid again put the same question to Chambers but this time in a different way so as to make him think under pressure “you didn’t choose that car at random did you Chambers, you had targeted that car didn't you, just tell me why?" he said this time in a raised voice and menacing way.

Chambers was in too much of a state to get the words out, he was sat crying and in agony, so Reid again tightened the vice a little bit, that was all that was needed, just the smallest alteration of the pressure of the vice felt to Chambers like his arm was going to explode as the bones and ligaments where slowly being crushed, the interior workings of his whole arm where now so squashed together that he had no control of any movement in his wrist or fingers.

This reaction made Pengilly protest and he begged Reid to show mercy, shouting over Chambers' screams, at Reid, but he was ignored, Russell remained silent and found it difficult to watch, so he faced away for most of the time, but neither they or anyone else listening could get away from the screams, which filled the air around them.

Tucker was standing facing the window inside the command centre, with her hands on her head, praying internally that Danks' men would be successful, Danks was staring wildly out of the window, listening in as the officers had reported that they had the window open and could now gain entry to the house he reported this news to Tucker who felt a small sense of relief from hearing it, Karen, who also heard the news of the officer's entry, was watching as she saw the window which was now wide open and the first officer climb into the room of the house with the other three about to follow.

Danks looked at tucker, "once they are all in and in position, do we have the order to move in?" he asked, Tucker didn't take long to think about it, she could hear the screams of a tortured

Chambers coming from over the phone, so she nodded at Danks "go in, and put a stop to this" she ordered, Danks immediately relayed this order to his team who confirmed they had received it.

In the cellar, and unaware that there where now four armed police officers just meters from him, Reid was feeling surprised that Chambers, with his skinny arms, had resisted this long, but was becoming increasingly frustrated at the lack of information he was getting from him, he leaned over close to his face "answer the question or on the next turn, I don't stop until the bones in your arm snap and crumble and turn to dust" he said menacingly "you will never be able to use that arm again, then I'll start on the other one" Reid informed Chambers' in a cold hearted way.

Karen, from her vantage point in the command centre, could now see that all four officers where in the house and she was fully aware that Tucker had given the order to move in, which gave her just seconds to act, as she listened on the phone to Reid asking chambers the question one last time, She heard a suffering Chambers beg Reid to stop "ok, please I'll tell you all you need to know, please stop" he shrieked out through the pain.

Karen knew that Reid had successfully broken Chambers at last but also that the armed response would be bursting in on the scene any second and regardless of whatever Chambers had to say, Reid would not be hearing it when the police crash in.

She had a dilemma, and with only seconds to decide what to do, she could hold off and let Chambers speak and hope that whatever he was about to say was the kind of information that

Reid was searching for, But if she did that, she knew that the cops would be inside the cellar with their weapons all pointed at Reid, and a strong possibility that at least one, if not all of them, would execute him, and since Reid was armed himself, she knew that he wouldn't be frightened to have a shootout, as it was what he was trained to do and would do it instinctively.

Or she could find a way to stop the assault and hope that Reid could still get Chambers talking some time later on, with so little time to make a firm decision she had to think on her feet and fast, and so with possibly just micro seconds to spare, she made her decision and acted on instinct. she leapt to her feet, before Reid could respond to Chambers, statement, "STOP" she screamed, everything seemed to pause,

Reid stopped the interrogation after recognising that it was Karen's voice shouting, Tucker looked at Karen and raised her hand to Danks to instruct him to stop his men, which he did via the radio.

All four officers, who were now inside a room of the house just opposite from the door way to the cellar door, froze immediately and remained perfectly quiet, each one wondering what was happening but being careful not to make any noise, even refraining from moving in case a creaky floor board could be heard over the sudden silence.

Karen could feel all the eyes of every officer in the place baring down on her "Steven, I think we could all do with a break" she said in a fumbled way, not really sure what she was about to say even while saying it, Reid knew there was something wrong but hadn't heard the safe word, so he gave Karen chance to say it in case there was a problem, Everyone's attention was now fixed on Karen, and the command centre, which a brief moment ago was filled with noises of chambers screaming, Reid shouting questions at him and the constant radio transmissions from the strike team, had now fell completely silent.

Karen, now feeling under the spot light, continued “Maybe you could give Chambers a drink, he might be more willing to talk if his mouth wasn’t so dry after all that screaming” she said nervously and fumbling her words “He could probably drink Niagara Falls” she continued in a desperate way to drag the safe word out, she knew very well that it wasn’t the slickest way to get it into conversation but she was in a major panic and she needed to say it quickly, in order to save Reid’s life.

Reid knew there was something wrong and now the safe word had been said he had to call a halt. “ok, let’s leave it there for a moment, I’ll give you time to breath and relax, before you can tell me what you know" Reid said, now wondering what was so wrong that Karen had called a halt just when Chambers was about to talk, "call me back in fifteen minutes" he said "I'll release Chambers from the vice and get him comfortable back on the table with his friends and we can all listen to what he has to say" Reid instructed, he hung up the phone and eagerly awaited Karen's call.

Karen, although feeling a sense of relief that she had managed to alert Reid, knew that she now had some questions to answer, and as she stood there looking at the phone, which was sounding the continuous tone of a disconnected line, she could feel Tucker staring at her, as well as the atmosphere which had become uncomfortable.

Tucker reached across and turned off the phone, which fell silent, the quietness within the room felt deafening as she walked from around the table and approached Karen "what the fuck are you doing?" she said abruptly to Karen, who was still flustered and trying to think on her feet "I couldn't take listening to that anymore, for Christ's sake, it was fucking barbaric" she shouted back at Tucker, in a manner that suggested that she had lost control of her temper and assuming that attack was the best form of defence in this instance.

Tucker, was still stunned at the sudden end to the call as well as stopping Danks' men storming the cellar, and she didn't take kindly to being shouted at by Karen, "there is nothing wrong with someone having a temper, but problems arise when that someone loses it" Tucker explained to Karen.

"I suggest you go outside and take a breath, in fact I suggest you remove yourself from this incident permanently" Tucker continued saying, who although was angry at the outburst, managed to say it in a low calm tone and remained in control.

Karen acted on Tuckers request, being ordered to leave had given her the perfect opportunity to ring Reid and inform him that he had trouble in the shape of four heavily armed police snipers just outside.

With everyone looking on, she walked out of the command centre and made her way to the edge of the cordon, getting her phone out of her pocket while she walked, again she had a quick look around before dialling Reid's number and waiting for him to answer, as she did she noticed her hand was shaking.

Reid, who had left Chambers still fastened in the vice for the time being, with his arm now feeling numb and it looked drained of colour, never bothered to move off the spot on this occasion to take the call from Karen, he felt that he had nothing to hide after Russell's little outburst earlier, and also felt that Russell wasn't so stupid to try anything like that again.

The phone rang, and Reid answered it before the first ring had ended "what's wrong?" he asked in an urgent tone, Karen spoke quickly and to the point "there are armed police outside the cellar door" she blurted out quickly.

Reid took a moment to let that information sink in, while Karen was expecting some kind of reaction "did you hear me?" she quickly asked Reid "There are four armed cops outside the cellar door" she repeated herself.

Reid never had chance to respond when the line went dead, Karen had hung up the phone as she didn't want anyone seeing her talking on it, she lit up a cigarette, took a long drag, inhaled and then exhaled the smoke with a satisfactory sigh of relief, secure in the knowledge that Reid could deal with the situation.

All she had to do now was get herself back inside the command centre and apologise to Tucker and hope she can remain on the team. Reid was left looking down at the phone in his hand, he knew that he had to deal with this situation carefully as well as immediately.

He placed the phone down onto the work bench and looked at Chambers who was slouched over, still with his arm in the vice, and then looked at Russell and Pengilly, who both stared back at him “don’t go anywhere” he said sarcastically “I just have something to do” he explained.

He then ran up the stairs toward the small landing, taking them two at a time, until he reached the top, he listened carefully with his ear pressed up against the door, the police men, who had silently made their way across the hall and where now standing outside the door, had no idea that Reid now knew they were there, but they all stood in total silence, all wondering why the cellar had suddenly fallen silent, Russell and Pengilly where left watching Reid, listening at the door with confused looks on their faces, not aware of what was happening.

After a few seconds Reid took a step back and faced the door, he took a breath and composed himself for a few seconds “Hey, I’m talking to the four policemen outside in the hall” he said loud enough for the police to hear, the four cops looked at each other, still remaining silent but not knowing what to do.

Reid waited for a few seconds for a reply of some sort which never came “oh for Christ sake lads, I know you’re there, so you might as well answer me” Reid said, again waiting for a response, but again the four men were frozen to the spot looking amongst themselves, not knowing whether to speak or not.

Reid decided to give it one more try “ok fella’s, since you’re not willing to talk, even though your cover has already been blown, this is what I’m going to do” Reid said talking through the door “I’ll count down from ten and if I get to the number one and you still haven’t answered me, I’ll shoot one of the hostages in the face, how does that sound?” Reid said knowing that the policemen could hear him.

The four police marksmen outside the cellar, had heard Reid loud and clear, and where now waiting for one of the others to speak first as they waited for Reid to start counting.

What they weren't aware of was that Reid was bluffing, he remained at the top of the stairs, and his pistol was still tucked into his belt line, he didn't want to shoot any of the three men, he still needed them, but it didn't stop Reid from building up a picture in their minds "I now have my gun aimed at the judge" Reid pointed out, "And it'll be him who gets it when I reach the count of one, is that clear boys" he said clearly enjoying this game of bluff "Ten, Nine, Eight, seven" Reid said slowly leaving a few seconds gap between each number, "Six, Five, four" he carried on, as he did he had contemplated what he would do if no one actually said anything, he considered firing a shot into the wall to make it look like he had shot the judge, but even as that idea entered his head he then thought the sound of a gunshot might send the police outside crazy and all hell could break loose.

However, he carried on counting, he got to number two when he heard a voice from the other side of the door "okay, okay, don't shoot anyone" was the response from one of the officers, the other three police couldn't really blame him for speaking out as they knew that their game was up.

Reid smiled to himself and felt that it was a little battle that had been won "wise move boys" replied Reid "there is a very small ground level window in this cellar, it is just big enough to see clearly out of and it faces the main gate" Reid said loudly through the door, "so you four have one minute to be walking, no actually, running through that gate, and if I don't see you then the consequences are on your head, is that understood?"

Reid instructed the four men, barking out the order reminiscent of his old army days.

The officers didn't hang around, and they didn't even bother to radio their control with the update that they were coming in, the rest of the team in the command centre and inside the cordon watched in amazement as they saw the four officers jogging back towards them, with no one knowing what had happened, Reid watched from the small square window in the cellar and saw the police snipers make a hasty retreat.

When they reached the command centre they were met by Tucker and Danks, "what happened?" asked Danks "he's been tipped off somehow" came the reply "He knew we were there and how many of us they were" one of the officers said, making himself spokesperson.

This information Danks found surprising, Tucker however, with a concerned look on her face, didn't, and she was seething at the lost opportunity, Tucker turned and walked back into the command centre, mulling over in her mind on how best to handle this situation.

CHAPTER TWENTY

Tucker was sitting at the table in the command centre, feeling quite forlorn, Reid had surprised her by phoning and she had just hung up the phone after speaking with him for just over a minute

He had shown great displeasure at her plan to storm the cellar with four heavily armed officers, Tucker had been honest, she pointed out that she wasn't prepared to sit by and listen to people being tortured, so that is the reason she instructed the strike team to move in.

It was at this point that Reid gave her some new information "hopefully there will be no need for anyone else to suffer, as long as Chambers tells the truth" he said with genuine hope in his voice.

He told Tucker to give him time to move Chambers back over to the main table with the others and to call back, to which Tucker had no choice to agree to.

It was at the point when she hung up the phone, when Karen walked back in, she had calmly finished her cigarette and hung back to watch what had happened with the armed response. She then left it a while as she knew that the fallout to Reid seeing off the four officers would be severe, and she wanted to give Tucker and Reid a chance to talk, knowing that Reid would contact her.

As she wandered back in she felt very nervous but hid it well, but before she had chance to speak Tucker stood up and instructed Karen to sit down, which she did, Tucker then banged on the window and waved for Grey, who was taking in some fresh air outside, to come in, Karen noticed the look on Tuckers face, it was emotionless, no smile or scowl but a look of a woman who had important business to attend to and wasn't about to let a thing like emotion get in the way.

Grey entered the room and as he did Tucker asked everyone else to leave, to the bewilderment of the half dozen people in there, they all hustled out leaving just Tucker, Karen and Grey inside "can I have a look at your phone please Karen?" Tucker said in a professional manner, Karen knew that it wasn't a request, even though it sounded like one, it was in fact an order.

"what do you want my phone for?" Karen replied, Tucker went straight to the point "because I've had my suspicions for a while now that someone is helping Reid and I think it's you" she replied with her eyes fixed on Karen the whole time, looking for any tell-tail signs that she may be guilty, making Karen feel very nervous.

Karen's mind was racing, she knew that when Tucker looked at her phone she would see that she had been calling Reid and she toyed with the idea of refusing, but she soon dismissed this idea as she knew that tucker would arrest her and then she would have to hand over her phone.

So not to prolong the agony, Karen slowly pulled her phone from her pocket and placed it on the table, "there is no point in searching through the call list" she explained "I have been helping Reid" she admitted to the stunned reaction from Grey "why?" he asked, Karen shrugged her shoulders "what does that mean, are you screwing him or something?" asked Grey, This infuriated Karen, so much so that she retaliated "No I'm not bloody screwing him you total cretin" she blasted back, Grey was about to enter into a full blown argument with Karen but Tucker raised her hand to him, quieting him immediately.

Tucker didn't want a shouting match as she knew that she would get no information from Karen that way, instead she sat down opposite Karen and in a calmer way asked Karen why she had helped a dangerous man like Reid.

"you call Reid a dangerous man" Karen replied, "But all he is, is a man who lost his wife in suspicious circumstances and never got justice" she said with her voice beginning to shake "the real dangerous men are in there with Reid" she continued saying.

Tucker was puzzled "who are you referring to, you mean Chambers?" she asked, the answer came as a surprise to Tucker, As Karen's eyes began to fill with tears "Chambers, in a way, but he is just a puppet, I'm talking about Bilton-Russell, He's the dangerous man" she said sadly.

Karen knew that after that comment, that she would have to open up on why she risked her career and her freedom in helping Reid, she looked at Tucker "you're a fair person, so I'm asking for a chance to explain" she said, Tucker nodded and then replied "of course"

Tucker, Grey and Karen sat around the table to talk, she told them both a story of when she was a young nineteen-year-old probationer constable with only nine months' service in the job, she was young and naive and had everything to learn, she was one of the prettiest females on the shift at the time and was receiving a lot of unwanted attention from a lot of the males on her shift, which she usually handled with a smile and laughed it off, referring to it as a joke, which in some cases it was.

As Tucker and Grey listened in on what was being said, Karen shook with emotion while telling some parts of it and her eyes filled with tears as she explained with such detail, that it was obviously deeply embedded in her memory, the tortured look on her face could be clearly seen as she was reliving every moment of her ordeal.

It was during a court appearance when an older male detective she was working with, who's name she refused to give, cornered her in a quiet corridor of an empty court room, one warm summer morning, Karen's tactic of fending off her admirers with a smile and treating it as a joke never worked on this man, who was more persistent than others she had come across.

He was a little bit more than an admirer, he had desires of a sexual nature towards Karen and was from an old school era where sexual remarks and inappropriate behaviour had been the norm and had been ignored for many years.

He was one of a handful of officers who still lived by that regime and as he was an extremely established detective he got away with a lot. He was of the impression that his thirty years' service gave him the power over her to make her fall prey to his advances.

He banked on the fact that her naivety and freshness to the job would help him get away with it, even if she complained, there were no witnesses, and she may even consent, which is what he was hoping, so in his mind it was worth the risk.

He completely ignored the fact that he was twice her age and overweight, and he was misogynistic, crude and arrogant, but his level of arrogance meant that he believed he was in with a chance.

He had been working alongside her for several weeks and he mistook her friendliness for tokens of some kind of attraction, so he chose the quiet moment out of the way in the corridor to make his move, which resulted in Karen rejecting him, even when Karen tried to push past this man he grabbed her and pressed her up against the wall and tried to kiss her, Karen's threats of reporting him where met with a laugh, "who would believe you over me" was the smiling reply from this sinister man.

She truly believed that she was going to be sexually assaulted that day, or worse, when out of nowhere, she suddenly felt her assailant being dragged off her, for a split second she never understood what had happened, one moment she was struggling to breath, as this man had his full body weight pushed against her as he attempted to kiss Karen, then suddenly he was sent flying backwards, when she looked, her knight in shining armour, was Oliver Bilton Russell, who stood there looking like a super hero to Karen, she watched as he verbally destroyed the male officer, she saw this man crumble before her eyes and it gave her a feeling of satisfaction, Russell never needed to use violence, all he needed was words and he used them so well that he cut the fat detective down to the floor piece by piece, word by word.

A shaken Karen felt a feeling of admiration for the handsome middle-aged barrister who sent the sleazy detective running from the court room in fear of his career and his liberty.

Against the advice from Russell, Karen never ever reported the incident for fear of reprisals and never told a soul, but she did agree to go out for dinner with the charming Russell, not knowing that he was a married man.

On the evening of the date, Karen had made a special effort, she wore a floaty summer dress and her hair was down, she was naturally pretty, never wearing much make up, and she was looking forward to her date with the successful and attractive knight in shining armour.

The date was spectacular, Russell picked her up in his Mercedes and they ate at a nice restaurant far out of town so no one they knew would see them, she never thought that anything was wrong with this, she just believed it when Russell pointed out that he liked his privacy.

After the date had finished they left the restaurant and a tipsy Karen got into the car, with Russell, they were still laughing and having a pleasant time.

It was on the journey home when things turned into a nightmare for Karen. Russell pulled into a dark and secluded car park in a wooded area, she questioned him on why he was doing this, but his whole demeanour had changed almost instantly, he had gone from charming and delightful to brooding and sinister in a matter of seconds and it scared Karen, it was as if he was two different people and suddenly she was trapped in a car with someone else, a man she didn't know.

Within a few seconds from entering the car park the car was parked up and the engine was switched off, and within a further few more seconds he was forcing himself on her, Russell, in one swift movement, had climbed over from the driver's side and placed his whole body on top of Karen.

She noticed as he swiftly climbed from the driver's seat over to the passenger seat, how with one hand, his belt was quickly un-buckled and his button and flies of his trousers where undone with speed and skill, like he had made that manoeuvre a hundred times before.

With one arm placed across Karen's chest, pinning her to the seat, his other arm climbed up inside her dress, his legs had been placed in between hers so stopping her from closing them he was fast and efficient with his moves, as if his skills in this type of scenario had been finely tuned over time.

Karen attempted to push him away from her, although Russell wasn't a big man, he was strong and with his whole-body weight on top of her she couldn't find the strength to force him away. "no, what are you doing?" she said in a panicked voice, but Russell didn't answer, he just had a wry smile to himself as if he was expecting the phrase, like he'd heard words like it said before. Now feeling pure terror Karen tried to wriggle out from under him, she could feel his hand getting further and further up her dress, Russell made it feel like it was part of the courtship, “resist, I like it the more they resist” he said panting with excitement “I always win” he boasted, it seemed like a challenge to him, as if when his hand made its way inside her underwear then the game was over, and she had to comply.

Karen’s heart was beating so fast that it caused her to sweat profusely, and she became short of breath, she tried to scream but she could barely find any air in her body to scream loudly, she hardly made any sound at all and therefore her screams for help went unheard, not just because there was no one around but simply because they were feeble and quiet.

She tried in vain to fight him off her once again, how could her dream date turn to such disaster? how could her knight become such a demon? These thoughts shot across her mind as she began to feel more and more helpless and began to wilt under his power.

Her eyes began to fill with tears as she felt his fingers enter her body, at that point her body involuntarily froze, and Russell gave her a smile "see, I always win" he whispered sinisterly as he moved his face closer and attempted to kiss her, Karen turned her head away a couple of times but it was then that Russell pulled her hair back and threatened "Stay still you bitch, I'm not playing now" he warned, his eyes were wide and Karen noticed the look of evil on his face.

As he moved in for a kiss again, with his fingers moving inside of her, Karen again tried to turn her head, Russell grabbed her hair more firmly this time and shouted in her face "do you want me to hurt you? you've lost, now stop moving" he screamed in her face, bits of his saliva landed on her face as he did, and Karen took the threat seriously, she feared for her life.

In complete fear Karen remained still, with tears running down her cheeks, With a quick pull, Russell had ripped her underwear from her body, and his trousers where moved down to below his knees in quick motion, the weight of his body on top of hers, helped in pinning her to the car seat, as she lay there the sweat from his brow dripped onto her face, she could smell his breath, she hadn't noticed anything wrong with his breath in the restaurant, as she hadn't been as close but now she could smell the stench of the garlic he'd eaten and the coffee he'd drank, that made her turn away, she had been attracted to the charming and polite persona which had rescued her from the clutches of that detective, but now he had become a depraved, vile rapist who was snaring her at this very point.

She felt him enter her body and she reacted to the pain which Russell seemed to enjoy, and showed it by saying "oh, yeah, that feels good" in a creepy self-satisfied way.

She felt sick as his hand moved up to expose and touch her breasts as he pushed himself deeper inside of her, making her wince and moan in pain again, every noise made by Karen made Russell more excited.

The more Russell became turned on the more vigorous he got, at one stage he lay thrusting himself inside of Karen with his hands pinning Karen's arms to her side, the feeling of control and power Russell enjoyed, and it made his selfish experience all the more satisfying.

The several minutes, the whole ordeal lasted, felt like hours for Karen, but it wasn't too long before Russell had ejaculated and suddenly the demon inside of him was gone, and a calm and somewhat embarrassed Russell climbed off her and began to dress.

It took half a minute before Karen realised it was over, she just laid there motionless, trying to regain control of her breathing which was quick and shallow as she had gone into shock.

She looked over at Russell with tearful eyes and saw him pulling his trousers back up, she began to straighten her clothes and never said a word. The silence made Russell feel uncomfortable "I'm not usually like that" he said in a quiet voice, Karen with a stunned expression found the courage to reply "usually like what, a rapist?" she replied, Russell glared at her, "Rapist?" he said questioning Karen "that wasn't rape, you where consenting" he told her "I mean that I'm not usually as rough, I apologise if it hurt" he added in a none sincere way, Karen was speechless that he actually believed that she was a willing partner, she saw that Russell had convinced himself of that, she felt violated and drained of emotion, so she stayed silent and let Russell drive her home without a single word being said between them.

Karen explained to Tucker and Grey that she couldn't remember entering her apartment when she got home, but that her next memory was of her standing in the shower, attempting to scrub herself clean, as she was doing so she knew it was the worst move to make as with every scrub of the sponge and with every drop of water that hit her body, she was washing away more and more evidence, but she couldn't be blamed for not thinking straight, all she felt at that time was the sickening feeling that her knight in shining armour, her super hero, had tricked her and was just another sleaze bag, in fact he was worse, he was a tactical rapist, a nasty predator right down to the bone, and she was just another prey.

That night and for a few nights following that harrowing ordeal, Karen never slept, and she never ate, she survived on only neat vodka that she felt numbed the pain and clouded her memory of that awful night.

She had to do a lot of soul searching, and come to terms with what had happened and what she was going to do, she lived alone and her family where hundreds of miles away, and she had no one to discuss it with, She was from out of town and hadn't been in the police force long enough to have built up any meaningful friendships so she had no confidents whose shoulder she could cry on, and who could give her the correct advice of what to do.

She took just one week off, claiming to have the flu, just so she could get her head together, before she returned to work. She spent that time at first doing what most people do who have suffered a trauma such as the one she had experienced, and that was blame herself.

In her drunken state she questioned herself and her choice of outfit she wore on that evening, was it to revealing? had she come across as a flirt? had she given out misleading signals? then, when sober, she would tell herself sternly that only one person was to blame and that was Russell, then she would get drunk again and the cycle would continue.

she never reported the rape as she believed that Bilton Russell would just say she had consented and she would be humiliated in court, plus she knew that an allegation like that against a top barrister would seriously damage her reputation and also her career.

So during a sober moment and with a clear mind she made the decision to put it in the box in her head marked insignificant, although in reality, she knew fine well that her inner voice wouldn't let that night become that and as the years wore on her overwhelming craving for revenge grew stronger and stronger.

With not reporting the rape she told herself that it may be naivety, fear or lack of experience or all of them but at that time she felt it was the right thing to do, she explained to Tucker and Grey that a part of her died that night and that she was never the same person again, she could no longer trust people and she rarely mixed with anyone socially.

It took all of Karen's inner strength to fight away the demons from that night and it took a lot of years for her to build up the strength to be able to become the strong woman she was now even though she still felt the anger and hatred sometimes.

Tucker sat shocked and open mouthed when she heard what Karen had gone through and she felt compelled to help her and also to tell Karen that she had gone the wrong way about getting justice for what had happened by getting Reid to drag Russell into a hostage situation.

Tucker reassured her that she would have Bilton Russell arrested once he was out of the cellar, but Karen pointed out that she never had him arrested all those years ago because she felt there was little chance of a prosecution, so there would be even less chance now, Karen also pointed out that it wasn't justice she was after "its revenge" she stated through the tears, wiping her eyes with a tissue supplied by Grey. "why look to get revenge now?" was the question Tucker was itching to get an answer too, Karen blew her nose, and wiped her eyes then looked at Tucker with a smile "because I know something that you don't" she said, her fists clenched with anger.

again, Tucker was left wanting "and what is that Karen?" Tucker asked, Karen sat back in her chair confidently, she had now regained her composure and she answered Tuckers question with confidence and a grin "when I arrested Chambers for the offence of killing Reid's wife, after hitting her with the car" Karen explained "He told me something when the tapes where off, that he would not repeat in court or to anyone officially, even though I tried to advise him to do so" Karen told an intrigued Tucker.

Tucker pleaded with Karen to explain what it was that she knew but Karen was keeping that secret safe until the right time "you will find out soon enough, and when you do, prepare yourself" she replied with a sly smile "then you will realise why I have gone to these extremes, Chambers wasn't prepared to do the right thing, so I felt I had too" Karen added.

Tucker felt that she couldn't leave it there "come on Karen, you're going to be arrested, so give me something" Tucker asked, "I'm just trying to understand why you did this" she explained.

Karen, knew that although the game was over for her, it wasn't over completely, and she had Reid, who was still in a strong position "I'll save it for the tape inspector Tucker" she replied, referring to her official police interview.

Tucker knew that she wasn't going to get anymore from Karen so pressed it no further, whatever the information that Karen was withholding was, she was doing so for a reason and she would have to wait to find out.

It was at this point that Tucker officially arrested Karen and read her the caution, making it official, Karen made no reply, but Tucker did have something to say "I can understand what you went through was beyond awful" she said sincerely "but I hope, for your sake, that all this that you have started, doesn't finish up with someone being killed" Tucker explained to Karen who sat motionless and expressionless as she listened to Tuckers words.

CHAPTER TWENTY-ONE

After the shock confession from Karen, who had been placed into the back of a police car, waiting to be taken away, Tucker was now back on the phone to Reid with the unenviable job of explaining why Karen was no longer there.

She was hoping that Reid would not react erratically and understand that Karen had in a sense played the game and lost, this, she hoped, might shake Reid up into realising that he too would end up the same way as Karen.

Reid was silent as he listened to Tucker explain what had happened, Staring at the phone as it laid flat on the work bench and with the others in the cellar listening to Tucker as she spoke to Reid with genuine feeling “I’m not sure how much you're aware of Steven, Karen never told me the full story or what parts of it that you know" Tucker explained "but she did give her reasons of why she wanted to help you and to be fair, although I do not and never will agree with what she did, I can understand why she did it" Tucker paused and both her and Reid sat for a few seconds and listened to the silence before she carried on "all I can tell you Steven, is what Karen said does change things a little and I fully intend to investigate further, and that's all I can tell you at the moment, but if you want to help Karen, your friend, it would be better for everyone if you gave yourself up now and let the hostages go" Tucker said in a sympathetic tone, hoping Reid would see her point.

Reid thought for a while which gave Tucker and the hostages hope that her words had made some sort of impact. Reid was contemplating if he could still achieve his main objective without Karen working for him on the other side, he was fully aware that he now had no one to warn him of the police's plans or how the police where feeling, if they were backed up against the ropes or what they were planning.

The lengthy silence became too much for Tucker to stand "Steven, are you still there?" she asked, Reid answered immediately confirming to Tucker that he was "where is Karen now?" he asked, "she is in our custody" Tucker replied, this answer frustrated Reid, as police terminology always seemed to, he always thought that the way the police talk was just a way of trying to make civilians feel inadequate, he felt the same about army slang but that wasn't as bad as the cops.

The way Reid saw it, there was no need for coded messages or pretentious phrases such as 'she is in our custody' or the most common one 'we have a man helping us with our enquiries' things like that just served to agitate Reid and he saw no benefit in it when you could simply say 'he or she has been arrested' “that’s not what I asked” Reid snapped, Tucker certainly didn’t want to make Reid angry, certainly not at this stage, so answered him in a way that she thought he wanted “right now she is sitting in the back of a car, waiting to be transported to the station” she answered.

“is she in handcuffs?” Reid asked. Again, Tucker wanted to appease Reid with her answers “we didn’t feel the need to cuff Karen” she replied, again silence fell but only for a few seconds. When it was broken by Reid, he had turned from a calm questioning man into army sergeant mode.

“good, I don’t want her in handcuffs, so make sure that she isn’t in them” he said speaking quickly “also, she goes nowhere, she is a part of this and she deserves to see it through to the end, and she will, so get her out of the car and sit her down next to you, she can observe the final outcome” Reid ordered, Tucker was taken by surprise by this request and tried to explain to Reid why this was not possible “Steven, she can have no further part in”…… Reid interrupted Tucker before she could finish “it’s not open for negotiation inspector, get it done now, or you will have a very angry man going crazy with a hand gun and explosives in a few minutes’ time, is that clear” Reid shouted down the phone, picking it up from the bench and holding it close to his face to enhance the effect.

Tucker knew that she had to do as Reid instructed, as Reid stayed on the line Tucker told Grey to go out to the car and get Karen, which he did without question.

Grey got to the car and explained to an astonished Karen that she was going back inside, the look of surprise on her face was plain for everyone to see, but it was soon followed by one of satisfaction as she knew that it was because of Reid who wanted her to witness the final part of their plan.

There was also a look of surprise on the faces of the on looking officers, who weren't privileged to the conversation between Tucker and Reid, they all stood outside and watched

Karen being lead from the car and back inside the command centre.

Karen and Grey entered the room and Tucker with a disapproving expression asked her to sit down, which she did "Karen is back in the room with us now Steven" she pointed out "welcome back Karen" Reid said, "I'm sorry for the situation that you've found yourself in" he said, his voice amplifying over the phones speaker.

Karen hesitated for a moment and looked at Tucker as if asking for permission to speak, the nod of her head Tucker gave her in return told her that it was fine “nothing I can’t handle Steven, so don’t blame yourself” Karen said, at this point Tucker felt the need to point out a few things “I want to make it clear Steven, that she is just here to observe, Karen has no role in this anymore” she said, looking at Karen the whole time.

Reid, who was eager to get things moving again replied simply be saying “understood and agreed” he then felt it was time to carry on with the interrogation, and prepared himself for work “is everyone at your end ready to take note of what is about to be said?” said Reid, who was now ready to go.

Tucker, with trepidation, confirmed that they were, and allowed for Reid to carry on but not before offering some advice aimed at the three hostages “I would advise the three of you to answer anything put to you, if you want to avoid being subjected to any pain” she said, hoping that the three men would take note.

Reid was quite surprised to hear such advice from Tucker, but hoped, along with Tucker, that they would take it “that’s good advice gentlemen, let’s go down the easy road for a change shall we” Reid advised as he positioned himself in front of Chambers, ready to make a start.

CHAPTER TWENTY-TWO

The scene was now set for what Reid saw as the final part of his plan, now that Chambers was aware of the lengths he was prepared to go to in order to get to the truth, Reid hoped that he would talk, with just the threat of torture hanging over him, after all, only a mad man would put himself through that kind of punishment again Reid thought.

Although Reid secretly admired Chambers' resilience for lasting as long as he did during the earlier torture session, he was certain that he would not want to experience anything like it again.

Chambers had been moved from the vice and back to the bench with Russell and Pengilly, his arm was in a bad way, some bruising was already beginning to appear along the forearm and around the wrist area showed a lot of swelling which suggested that there may be a broken bone or two.

It was causing him a lot of pain with a dull continuous ache, mixed shooting pains which shot along his arm all the way to his fingertips whenever his arm was moved, which Chambers found to be excruciating.

It was especially painful when his arm was cable tied to the bench again by Reid, as he let out several cries because of the pain, giving Reid the opportunity to show Chambers and the others exactly how much he didn't care for their welfare with the odd comment.

With a shake of the head Reid gave an ultimatum “which would you prefer, vice or table?” he asked, already predicting the answer, but still wanting to hear it come out of Chambers’ mouth anyway.

Chambers never answered but cried and sniffed and yelped as the cable ties where fastened tightly by Reid. As Chambers found out earlier, Reid didn’t like to be ignored, Chambers’ mind was on other things like the pain in his arm and Reid’s question hadn’t really registered, but Reid made it register when he repeated it whilst giving his injured arm a slight squeeze as he did “do you want to stay here or go back on the vice?” he asked a second time,

Chambers screamed out in pain as the pressure of Reid’s grip felt like his arm was back in the vice again and he spat out the answer quickly so that Reid would stop “here, I want to stay here” he shouted through the agony.

As Reid had hoped, he did not want to be tortured again and he gave him a quick talk, pointing out that he was prepared to do a lot more should he decide not to talk, this warning was met with a rapid succession of nods from the head of Chambers plus verbal confirmation “I’ll tell you everything, I don’t care anymore” Chambers responded in desperation.

However, being a barrister, Russell couldn’t help pointing out a few facts to Reid “whatever he tells you will be inadmissible in a court of law” he said with delight.

Reid didn’t respond, instead he just positioned himself in front of Chambers and prepared to hear what he had to say, Russell however wasn't quite finished "he's been physically tortured for Christ sake, he could tell you that he wears his mother's clothes every Friday, but because you've tortured him while saying it, it doesn't mean it's true" he pointed out, trying to get through to Reid.

Again, Reid wasn't interested in what Russell was saying, even when Tuckers voice was heard over the phone reinforcing that opinion, he still never took notice "he's right Steven, why don't you let me re-interview him under caution and at least then it's done the right way, according to law" she was heard saying, which brought a smug look to Russell's face.

At this point, Pengilly decided to have his say "this entire thing has been a waste of time, all you've done is get yourself a very hefty prison sentence simply because you didn't agree with the verdict in court" he said.

It was this comment that made Reid retaliate, "the court case was rigged, and you know it" he said, directing his comment to Pengilly, this in turn made Pengilly answer him back immediately "there was no rigging, no fixing, not in my court room, I can assure you of that" he said forcefully, defending not only his credibility but his reputation as well.

Reid, for the first time, felt that Pengilly might have a point, it wasn't so much what he said but the way he said it, it was a comment said with passion and it sounded like it was said with true belief, he looked over at the judge, who looked right back at Reid "I promise you Mr Reid, there is never any foul play in any of my court rooms" Pengilly said, sensing that Reid was finally beginning to listen.

Russell looked at Pengilly then glanced over at Reid as he sat opposite Chambers, and now staring down at the floor as if in thought, Pengilly, felt that he was getting somewhere, even Tucker, without the benefit of being able to see what was happening, could feel a shift in the mood, just by listening in on the phone, so she allowed the conversation to carry on without interruption.

Russell carried on looking at Pengilly, wearing an expression that was willing him on to say more of the same things in an attempt to win Reid over, Pengilly read the situation and decided to carry on with a little more "you see son, that's why we have had the courts in this land for hundreds of years" He said, with his confidence rising "it's a place of fairness, of trust and of honesty" Pengilly finished off saying, this brought a reaction from Reid, but one that Pengilly and the rest where not wanting, Reid got to his feet and walked towards the stairs, with his back to the three men he spoke, "have you ever been lied to in your court room judge?" Reid asked, Pengilly was trying to play safe, he felt that any wrong word or sentence could harm the situation, so he wanted to keep things honest, he knew Reid was clever enough to recognise bullshit "I honestly don't know" he said being as honest as he could be, Reid kept his back to the three "the answer is yes judge, we established that earlier" he replied.

This left Pengilly a little off balance as he didn't know what he was referring to, Reid turned around slowly and faced the men "don't you remember, you were told in court that Chambers had completed a detox programme and was now drug free, but he's obviously suffering from drug withdrawal while being down here, so that's obviously a lie" Said Reid with a look of satisfaction.

Pengilly answered in the only way he knew how to "I'll be honest" he said, "that was a lie and one that was told by Chambers' counsel in order to help his cause in court" he replied showing a look of disappointment.

Reid was now ready to spring the trap that he had been leading Pengilly into "so how many more lies have been told by his counsel to help his cause in court?" he said, then waited for a reply, which never came, instead all Reid saw was a look of disdain on Pengilly's face which was directed at Russell.

With his point made Reid sat down again in front of Chambers, he cracked the knuckles of both hands and prepared to get to the truth, he knew that Tucker and Karen where listening in and that all this was close to an end, but only if Chambers talked and told the truth.

With a calm approach Reid addressed Chambers “okay Craig, a little while ago, you were about to tell me why you stole my wife’s car” He spoke slowly and in a befriending way “do you remember that?” he asked, Chambers replied with a nod and a gulp, Reid sat back in his chair “carry on” he said.

Before Chambers could utter one syllable Russell laughed out loud, prompting a response from Reid “something funny pal?” Reid asked, Russel shook his head as if in disbelief “yes this, all of this, is what’s funny, in fact it’s not even funny, its more tragic” he said in a dismissive tone,

Reid stared at him “I don’t care what you think, now shut up” he replied, Russell however wasn’t going to “so let me get this correct, whatever he is about to tell you, you’re going to believe are you?” asked Russell, Reid was becoming increasingly agitated at the interruptions and just turned away from Russell and indicated with a nod of the head to Chambers to carry on.

Chambers took a breath, and whilst wincing with the pain in his right arm he looked down at the table "I was paid money to steal that car" he admitted, Reid's attention was suddenly held "for what reason?" he asked, Chambers didn't answer, with his head lowered he began to cry.

Karen, sitting in silence in the command centre could hear every word being said, in her mind she was willing Chambers to talk and to tell all, but all she could hear was sniffling coming from over the phone, she sat a while longer until she could not hold her counsel any longer "tell him Chambers, for god's sake tell him what you told me" she shouted out, Tucker responded angrily "shut up DC Caswell or I will have you removed" she shouted back at Karen, Reid, upon hearing this became more intrigued with what Chambers had to say “speak Chambers, now” he ordered, he reached across the table and gently placed his hand onto the right arm of Chambers, Chambers panicked and looked up quickly at Reid, shaking his head “no, please don’t hurt my arm” he pleaded with Reid, who stared at Chambers, a cold icy stare that went right through Chambers, scaring him and cutting into his soul “it was a hit” a shaking Chambers screamed through the tears, this left Reid dumbfounded as to why someone would want Rebecca dead “why?” he asked sharply.

When Chambers’ answer had stalled Reid squeezed his arm just slightly, it was enough to cause Chambers an immense amount of pain and he screamed out “she was pregnant” he yelped through the agony, Reid could hardly believe his ears “tell me more” he shouted back “SPEAK” he screamed, as he felt the anger beginning to rise from the pit of his stomach.

Chambers was to scared and in too much pain but through the torture he managed to say two words that grabbed Reid's attention as if he had been grabbed by the scruff of the neck "ask him" was the reply from Chambers, as he looked over towards Russell who had an astounded look on his face "he knows" chambers added now shaking so much his voice tremored.

Russell gave a smirk as if reaffirming his earlier warnings that whatever Chambers said wouldn't be worth listening to "I have no idea what the hell he is talking about" was Russell's reply with a light-hearted tone.

Reid was not the kind of man to dismiss such information so easily and he rose from his seat and approached Russell, whose reaction suddenly change when he realised that Reid was taking the comment seriously "what the hell is he talking about?" Reid asked Russell with a glare, Russell laughed out of nervousness "how the hell do I know; do you remember when I said that you cannot believe anything a tortured person says?" he asked Reid panicking, Reid asked him again "I said, what is he talking about" he repeated this time in a menacing way, his face contorted with the anger that was building up inside of him.

Russell was now fighting for his safety, he was used to thinking on his feet and used to thinking quickly, but the pressure cooker of this situation made it difficult for him to think straight "look, you cannot trust this man, he is trying to set me up, so you will leave him alone, can't you at least understand that?" he replied quickly and with hope that Reid would side with him and see his point.

Reid suddenly stopped, something inside of him clicked into place like a final piece of a jigsaw, he suddenly realised something that was now so obvious, he wondered why he hadn't thought of it before, he calmly walked back to his seat and carried it over to where the vice was located and sat down near it.

"how much do you charge to defend someone?" he asked Russell, the sudden change of subject threw him for a moment, so much so that he wasn't sure how to answer the question "what has that got to do with anything?" Russell asked back, Reid was determined to get an answer "I'll ask one more time, then I'll put your arm in the vice" he said, "how much do you earn?" he said slowly, Russell never hesitated "between three hundred and five hundred pounds" he replied, "per hour?" Reid asked,

Russell was feeling like he was on the back foot but could not work out why he was being asked these questions all of a sudden “yes, per hour, what has this got to do with anything?” he blurted back at Reid.

Reid sat back in his seat and seemed to relax for a second “then how did a piece of shit like chambers afford to have you defend him?” he asked, he happily accepted the long pause that came after the question as Russell realised that he never had a solid answer for it.

Russell’s face told a story, one of a clever, educated man who had just been tripped up, just been outplayed at his own game, by a man with less than half the qualifications that he had, A man with Russell’s ego found this hard to deal with and therefore, answered in an avoiding way “that is between me and my client” he said quite pathetically.

Reid read from that answer all he needed to know and that was Russell was in this up to his neck, Russell, although now genuinely flustered, tried in vain to hold it together "look I have no idea what my earnings have to do with this, or how Craig can afford my services" Russell said in desperation he pointed over at Chambers who was staring at him venomously "what I do know is that he has fooled you, and put blame on me, and you've fallen for it" Russell carried on saying.

Reid was very used to putting the pressure on people he had to get information out of, at certain times the best way to get people to talk was by saying nothing, sometimes the loudest man in the room was the one who says nothing, and Reid proved it by remaining quiet, which was worrying for Russell.

As Reid sat quietly just looking at Russell with no expression on his face, Russell's heart was beating fast and he felt the sweat running down his face and also down his back, he began to talk in the hope that his chosen words would somehow convince Reid that he was barking up the wrong tree.

“look, Steven” Russell said, pleading with Reid, “all I know for certain is that Chambers is a known liar, he’s a rat, he’ll lie and cheat to get himself out of a hole and that’s what he is doing now” he carried on saying, Reid never replied but maintained the expressionless look toward Russell, which he found unnerving.

Russell, tried again to get through to Reid “I can tell you, I can give you my word, on my honour, I had nothing to do with your wife’s death” Russell pleaded “you can put my arm into that vice and tighten it until my arm snaps and I’ll say the same thing” he said with conviction.

This time, upon hearing those words, Reid reacted "you protest too much, Oliver" was Reid's reply, he rose from his seated position, bent over the tool box and dipped his hand inside "I don't have time for the vice" he said, as he stood up he was holding the secateurs in his hand, he quickly marched over to Russell, went behind him and grabbed hold of his left arm, The first time Russell got a clear look at what Reid was holding in his hand was when he felt and saw the jaws of the cutters being placed tightly around his little finger, he began to panic and plead with Reid "No, please, no don't do this please" said Russell, very close to tears, Reid had the power, and Russell knew it, "start talking or lose it" Reid said, Russell was beginning to shake but still maintained his story "I swear to you, I'm innocent" was his reply.

There was one second between Russell finishing that sentence that seemed to take for ages then the other two men in the cellar heard a quick snap, as Reid placed instant pressure on the handles of the cutters, the sharp powerful blades cut through the flesh of Russell's finger like a hot knife cut through butter, and then a millisecond later the same steel blades snapped through the bone of Russell's little digit as if it was a dry twig. At first Russell reacted with shock at seeing his finger fly off his hand and across the table, landing on the cold dirty floor, just for that brief moment Russell felt no pain, but then the shock factor dissolved as quickly as it had arrived and Russell's screams of agony where ear piercing, as the blood from his severed finger dripped onto the table, Pengilly turned away close to vomiting, Reid looked at chambers and the once crying timid man was watching Russell's reaction with a strange look of satisfaction on his face.

Amidst Russell's whimpering Reid hadn't finished and he grabbed the same hand which was covered in thick dark red blood, it made it slippery to keep hold of as Russell began to struggle, but Reid managed to get the jaws of the cutters tightly around his middle finger.

Russell was crying and begging for mercy, the listening Tucker, Grey and Karen could hear the cries and screams but did not know that Reid was cutting the fingers off Russell, Even Tuckers protests either could not be heard over the phone or where being ignored.

Reid Gave him one chance "Tell me what you had to do with my wife's death, and do it now" he said, meaning every word, Russell knew that Reid was willing to cut off every single one of his fingers if he didn't speak, he was a beaten man, fully aware of who was listening he knew he had to tell the truth.

His words where sometimes difficult to hear through the whimpering and the tears but he started to tell Reid all he knew "we were having an affair" he blurted out over the pain "we had been for eight months, and then she told me she was pregnant" As Russell spat out the words, and Reid listened, it felt like he had been stabbed through the heart for Reid "carry on" he demanded.

Russell did as requested "she was going to leave you, she wanted me to leave my wife and to be with her" he carried on saying, his words broken and interrupted through the tears and the gasping for breath, Reid still needed more and demanded it with the threat of tightening the jaws of the cutters, this made Russell yelp and throw out more information, that was becoming increasingly difficult for Reid to hear.

“she was going to ruin me, I said I couldn’t leave my wife as she would take over half of what I had” Russell explained as best he could “but she said she would tell my wife about the affair, and keep the baby” Reid was left devastated, he moved the cutters away from Russell and dropped his hand, the cellar fell quiet and Reid walked slowly around the table and back to the chair he had been sitting on.

No one spoke for a minute, the listening police also sat quiet, waiting for some voice or sound to come from the cellar, but nothing came. As Reid sat slumped in the chair, still holding the cutters, the blood of Russell dripping onto his jeans, Pengilly broke the silence “I don’t understand, why kill the girl?” he asked Russell, there was more silence as Russell refused to answer.

It was Chambers this time who spoke out “he hired me, I was put in touch with Russell through a friend” he said, “I was told that a very rich man wanted a woman to be killed and to make it look like an accident" Chambers went on to say.

As Chambers was talking Reid rose from his chair and walked to the stairs feeling numb, he climbed half way up them then sat down on a step slowly "carry on" he said softly, Chambers told Reid and the Tucker how he and Russell had met secretly and that it was Russell's idea, Russel and Chambers had been driving around for hours following Rebecca Reid as she visited friends, it was during her visit to her friend in the country that Russell told Chambers to get out of his car as this would be the time he would steal he car.

He was to make sure that he didn't start the engine until she was outside, being a barrister and priding himself on knowing how people think and act he banked on the feisty Rebecca trying to stop her car being stolen, Chambers was instructed to drive towards her if she attempted to stop her car being stolen, and if she did he was to run her over, making sure that she was hit hard enough that she was killed.

The plan worked perfectly well, Rebecca ran out into the road and Chambers, as instructed by Russell, ran her over, at that point Russell drove away, unseen, but Chambers was told to stop at the scene and wait for police, he was to act shocked and to give the police the story that he told in court.

He Was to be helpful to the police and not interfere with the investigation at all, all he had to do was stick to the story that Russell had created, and all would work out well, he was told that a small amount of prison time could be expected but upon release that he would be handsomely rewarded.

As the story was being told, Tucker looked over at Karen who looked back at her and nodded "I told you" she mouthed at Tucker.

Chambers was given assurances that he would be defended by Russell in court, who would use his skills to get him off lightly as he did and that he would be paid more money than he had ever earned in his life for his work, half would be paid in cash upon the job being done and the other half after his release from prison.

Reid sat on the stairs, for the first time since the start of this ordeal he looked a broken man, he had no answer to the news he had just heard, he was risking everything for the woman he loved, he knew she had been murdered, he felt it in his heart and he wasn't going to rest until he had gotten justice for her.

But what he didn't know was why he was recruited by Karen, when during a silly moment, because of lack of sleep and the pressure put on him by Karen under questioning, he told her of Russell's involvement in the whole thing when the tapes had been switched off, in a gloating way, he thought that without proof Karen could not use the admission in court, And he was right, but he hadn't known of Karen's hatred and her past with Russell, and if it hadn't had been for that gloating at the end of the interview, they would have got away with it.

Reid was sitting slumped over on the stairs, as he listened to every word he felt his heart break more and more, he wished he could have just one minute with Rebecca to ask just one question "why?" he wasn't aware she was having an affair with Russell, he thought they were happy, they had been together a long time and he looked at her like his soul mate, his life partner and that she felt for him the same as he felt for here as the pain in his heart grew and grew he wiped away his tears and sat upright “how much?” he said without looking at anyone, just staring straight ahead at the wall at the foot of the stairs.

The room fell silent, until Pengilly broke the silence “do you mean how much was Chambers paid?” he asked, Reid took a breath and then as if he had re-energised himself he jumped to his feet and walked down to the bottom of the stairs and stood facing the three men “that’s right judge” he said “how much money was my wife’s life worth?” after asking the question he glanced over at Russell, he quickly made the assumption that he was in no fit state to answer any more questions, he was slumped over the table, still crying with a small pool of blood, from his severed finger forming on the table in front of him.

Reid turned and looked at Chambers “six Grand” he answered, “three before, and I was due to get another three when I got released” he admitted.

Reid was astounded “six thousand pounds” he repeated, “that is how much you were paid to kill my wife, the woman who I loved with every fibre of my being” Reid muttered quite calmly, until only seconds later he could feel his anger building as these facts suddenly hit home.

with his fists clenched Reid screamed at the top of his voice “SIX FUCKING GRAND” he bellowed like an out of control demon, he swung his mighty right fist into the face of Chambers, immediately on impact spatters of blood landed on the wall behind him and two teeth where spat out of his mouth along with the thick red blood from the crevices of the gums they were once attached to.

Reid’s face showed the deep routed pain that he was feeling, he was concerned as he felt that he could barely hold it together, with his eyes reddened from the tears he was uncontrollably crying he slowly walked to the table to where the phone was laying and picked it up, leaving Chambers unconscious and slumped forward on the table.

He held the phone up to his mouth “did you hear all of that inspector Tucker?” he asked, Tucker responded with heartfelt dignity “yes we did Steven” she said, “I can guarantee you that this case will be re-opened and Chambers and Russell will be arrested” she finished off saying.

Reid had one more thing to say “Karen?” he said softly, Karen looked at Tucker who nodded to her, allowing her to Speak “I’m here Steven” she replied, herself feeling the emotion of the admission and the pain of Reid, a man she considered her friend.

Reid, who was now a broken man and whose voice quivered, managed to get his words out "Thank you, for what you did" he said, Karen with a gulp simply replied, "you're welcome" before adding "you deserved to know the truth".

Reid looked around one last time at the devastation he had caused over the few hours he had been there, and all to get to the truth, he wasn't to know that the truth would hurt him so much. He spoke into the phone one last time "tell your snipers that I'm coming out the front door, I'm unarmed so there will be no need to shoot" he told Tucker.

With a huge sigh of relief Tucker picked up a radio and relayed that information to Danks and his team, Reid looked down at the silver wedding band on his finger, he had a quick flash back to the day that Rebecca placed it on his finger, and promised to love him forever and to always be true to him, he slowly removed it and placed it into his pocket “I know a place where I can put this” he said to himself, Reid then turned and began to walk up the stairs, as he got half way up he stopped and turned to face the three men “you’ll be safe down here until they come for you” he said, Pengilly was the only one to acknowledge him with a nod of the head.

Reid looked at Pengilly “I owe you an apology judge, it turns out that you had nothing to do with all of this” he said with a sad heart.

Again, Pengilly gave him a reassuring nod of the head, just before he started to walk up the stairs, he again stopped and spoke to Pengilly “earlier, when I smashed the wine Judge, you said id shown myself for the man I was, what did you mean?” he asked, Pengilly thought carefully for an answer “well at that moment, I thought you were a thug, a common vandal” he replied “but now I know that you’re a man who is simply in pain, and I’m very sorry for what you have learned here today” Pengilly added, Reid didn’t answer, he just turned and walked slowly up the stairs, Pengilly watched as he reached the top, unlocked the door and disappeared through it.

Leaving Pengilly to survey his surroundings, as the cellar fell silent he could still hear the dripping and splashing of the wine as it dropped from the rafters and he watched as it ran down the walls, he looked closely at the pieces of shattered glass that were once wine bottles as they littered the floor of the cellar along with the destroyed shelving units.

He then shook his head in disappointment when he saw Russell sitting forwards crying with self-pity and noticed the missing finger and the pool of blood that covered the table, he then looked past Russell and saw Chambers with blood pouring out of his mouth as he was sat forward still out cold from the punch he had taken.

After the seconds it took to take all of that in Pengilly sat Back in his seat and glanced up towards the ceiling “thank god that’s over” he said out loud.

CHAPTER TWENTY-THREE

Reid stood in the hallway of the house, still devastated from the news he had received earlier, the pained look on his face was plain to see, he took a couple of deep breaths as if composing himself for what was to come.

He calmly walked to the kitchen, situated to the left of where he was standing, he crouched down and made his way to the window, from his crouching position he carefully raised up so his eyes where level with the windowsill and peered out to the large garden, he was surprised to see no armed police; it wasn't until he furthered his gaze to the surrounding forest that he spotted four snipers hiding amongst the greenery, he shook his head in disbelief "if you boys had been trained by the army, I wouldn't be looking at you right now" he muttered to himself.

Reid then wandered back out of the kitchen still in his crouched position and back out to the hallway, he pulled out a remote control from his pocket, it was small, the size of a mobile phone, and it was rudimentary, with only three switches on it and held together with black electrician's tape.

It was obviously self-made by Reid, but it was only to serve one purpose and that purpose was soon to be utilised in a moment.

Back in the command centre Tucker had ceased communications with Reid by telephone and had told her armed response team to be on alert as Reid was coming out, she stood outside the centre along with Karen and the others and waited for some kind of movement from within the house, she expected to see the front door open any second with Reid standing there with his hands up.

Tucker was more nervous now than at any other time during the siege, she noticed that it had become eerily quiet and she was uneasy at the amount of time that Reid was taken to surrender himself. What she was praying for was an easy surrender and not for Reid to come out firing, it was obvious to her that Reid was now a very hurt man after hearing the truth of what happened to his wife and maybe he felt he had nothing to live for and decided to come out guns blazing, Tucker knew that he wouldn't stand a chance against so many police marksmen with their rifles trained on the house and she knew that Reid would know this too, but she could only see two ways for this to go, Reid would either come out and give himself up peacefully, which is what she was hoping, or he'd come out firing which would be suicide. In Tuckers opinion there was no other way that it could go.

Reid, still inside the house by now had switched on the remote control with a flick of a switch, a little red light shone brightly on the end to alert him to the fact that the equipment was live.

He opened the door to the cellar and stepped inside onto the small landing, closing the door behind him, the three hostages were still tied to the bench, Chambers was beginning to come around and was groaning and Russell and Pengilly sat silently watching him, wondering what he was doing. Reid gave them a nod and a smile then mouthed the word "BOOM" as he flicked the second switch on the remote control.

Within one second there was a massive explosion, so powerful that dust and rubble fell from the ceiling of the cellar and the house shook. Outside, the explosion took the police by surprise causing some of them to dive to the ground for cover, Tucker looked on as she witnessed the entire front of the house explode, every window shattered into pieces as flames roared from the window frames, the explosion was so fierce that part of the front of the house collapsed with the extreme force of the bang.

The explosion shook the very ground beneath them, Tucker grabbed her radio “someone let the fire brigade through the cordon now” she shouted over the noise of the mayhem that had ensued.

The marksmen at the back of the building who heard and felt the blast where suddenly on red alert, and on their feet, not knowing what to expect, Reid and the three hostages were still safe and well inside the cellar, Reid coolly flicked the third switch on the remote and this time the rear of the building explode in similar fashion to the front had.

Again the police outside where surprised at the second explosion, the four marksmen at the rear of the house all dived for cover in the forest as debris was sent flying towards them, some of which was burning, setting fire to bushes and trees that they were using as cover, just like the explosion at the front of the house, every pane of glass shattered, and part of the premises collapsed with the force of the blast.

Reid heard the second blast as it went off and had to time his next move perfectly well, as the explosion had caught everyone's attention he darted from the cellar and ran towards the back of the house, amidst the explosion and resounding fireball that it created.

It looked like he had ran into the flames, as he did he disappeared from view. The snipers who were now getting to their feet never saw Reid or any movement inside the house either before or after the explosion.

Out the front of the house the fire brigade where now in attendance after being on standby outside the cordon for so long and where dealing with the house which was now engulfed in flames.

This was being witnessed by Tucker and the others as they all looked on quietly at the burning wreckage of the building that Reid had created.

CHAPTER TWENTY-FOUR

It wasn't too long before the fire fighters had the flames under control and parts of the building had been extinguished leaving just charred remains and wreckage, a search and rescue team had entered the house when it was safe.

Pengilly, Russell and Chambers had been located down in the cellar, inside the concrete casing they had all been protected from the blast and apart from the damage to them that Reid had inflicted they were totally unharmed from the explosion.

All three men were given medical treatment especially Chambers and Russell, and Tucker took great pleasure in arresting both men with a smiling Karen in the background as she watched on to see Bilton-Russell, in such pain and looking a beaten man being officially cautioned and arrested for murder and rape.

Karen’s feeling of satisfaction was more than she could have hoped for, Reid had taken everything from this man, and with her help, Russell had lost his valuable wine collection, his marriage and his house, and also his job and his freedom, Karen, even though she was still under arrest herself, allowed herself to feel content and happy for the first time in a long time.

Tuckers main concern now was finding Reid, as the search teams scoured the wreckage of what was once a very nice house, parts of which were still burning, she stood outside the command centre with radio in hand, waiting on news of the teams either finding Reid’s body or finding him trapped under the rubble.

She waited for over an hour, Karen, Chambers and Russell had been taken away, Pengilly had gone to hospital and most of the team had left, but Tucker remained, eager to find out what had happened to Reid, but no news came.

Tucker looked at the state of the building, it was demolished and a black charred wreck, in parts, where it had collapsed, it was difficult to tell what type of building it once was.

Reid had planted the explosives in such positions that it ripped through the main structure of the house, thus causing so much damage, But Tucker could not see how Reid would have

survived the blast unless he was in the cellar along with the others, but according to what she had now been told, Reid wasn't in the cellar, so she intended to wait at the scene until his body was found and she was informed by the chief fire investigations officer that if Reid was outside the cellar when the house exploded, he would most certainly be dead, and they would find his remains eventually.

This news made Tucker quite remorseful, she had come to respect Reid, especially now that she was aware of why he had done all of this, she wanted him to be alive, she was most definitely going to arrest him if he was, but she felt that a man such as him, who was prepared to give everything and anything in order to get to the truth, deserved to live and to have his day in court and not to have perished in the flames

CHAPTER TWENTY-FIVE

The rain had now stopped, but had left the grass in the cemetery soggy and quite slippery, there were a few people wandering around, some walking too graves, some walking away and some attending to graves. As the sun began to break through the clouds, it shone a beam of warm sunlight onto a black granite headstone, which displayed the name of Rebecca Jane Reid in gold writing.

It had the usual information, her date of birth and the day she died, how she was a loving daughter and wife and sister and how she had been taken from her family prematurely. It was no different to any of the other headstones in the cemetery.

Below the writing and resting up against the headstone were several bouquets and wreaths which had been left by family and friends as a mark of respect.

About a foot away from the headstone, on the grave itself, lay a single white rose, around the stalk of the rose was a silver wedding band, the one Reid wore on his wedding finger and the one he had taken off in disgust at finding out the truth.

Upon doing so Reid had muttered to himself that he had a place for it. Maybe this grave was that place.

THE END.

Acknowledgements

Wendy, for her encouragement and support.

...

Charlie without whom this wouldn't have been possible.

...

Caroline Senior, Thank you for giving me the key to your home and to my success.

Printed in Poland
by Amazon Fulfillment
Poland Sp. z o.o., Wrocław

Where to watch Game
IN THE
KRUGER NATIONAL PARK

BY NIGEL DENNIS

First published 2000

2 4 6 8 10 9 7 5 3
Sunbird Publishing (Pty) Ltd
34 Sunset Avenue, Llandudno, Cape Town, South Africa

Registration number: 4850177827

Publisher Dick Wilkins
Consultant Marc McDonald
Editor Brenda Brickman
Designer Mandy McKay
Maps John Hall
Production manager Andrew de Kock
Reproduction by Unifoto (Pty) Ltd, Cape Town
Printed and bound by Tien Wah Press (Pte) Ltd, Singapore

ISBN 0 624 03885 8

CONTENTS

INTRODUCTION

Rooibosrant Dam near Bateleur Bushveld Camp in the Shingwedzi region is a prime spot to observe the Park's aquatic birds.

The Kruger National Park is considered to be one of the greatest game parks in the whole of Africa. In fact, few national parks in the world can offer visitors the same opportunity to view such a rich diversity of animal species. However, as game is never evenly distributed in the Park, there can be no guarantee of the sighting of any particular animal in any particular spot. This guide to game-viewing – a compilation of information supplied by section rangers and other Kruger staff, as well as my own observations – is intended to substantially increase prospects of viewing game in Kruger.

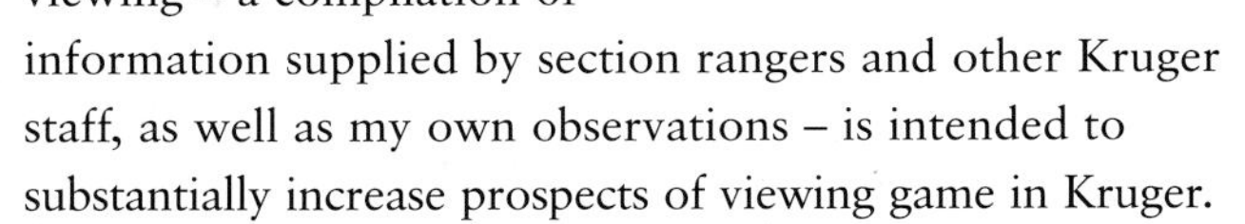

As a wildlife photographer, I have been a regular visitor to the Park over the past decade. As a result, I have driven some of the routes through Kruger a hundred times or more. It is my belief, based on experience, that, by following the general game-viewing hints offered here, and by concentrating on the prime routes indicated on the area maps provided in this book, game-viewing experiences will be significantly enhanced.

SEASONS AND CYCLES

Game movements and concentrations in the Kruger Park are greatly influenced by the availability of surface water. The Kruger Park experiences a dry season from May through to October. Although these winter months are generally considered the best for game-viewing, the timing of animal movements is dependent on the amount of rainfall that fell during the previous summer. After a very wet summer, movements to areas surrounding rivers and dams usually occur late in the winter, making September the most consistently rewarding viewing period. In times of drought, these animal concentrations around water can begin as early as May or June, with a game-viewing bonanza continuing through until the first spring rains.

While the winter season is the most productive in terms of the numbers of species sighted, the Kruger summer also has its special attractions. Impala lambs are born in November and December, and migrant birds also peak at this time. Even the late summer period, when long grass makes most game-viewing difficult, may be especially rewarding, particularly after an overnight shower. An early morning game drive under these conditions may well produce sightings of lion and leopard, as they are averse to walking in long, wet grass, and so prefer to use roads for hunting activity.

As a general rule, it is not a good idea to spend long hours alongside water holes in summer-rainfall months, as the numerous natural pans throughout the Park will hold water, and game will be well dispersed. It is, therefore, better to cover as much ground as possible.

Aside from the seasonal variation in rainfall, Kruger also undergoes cycles of wet and dry periods, lasting several years. Although numbers of most species increase during wet cycles, with abundant browsing and grazing opportunities, as well as surface water surpluses, the winter concentrations of game are less pronounced. On top of this, the long grass and thick bush that covers much of the Kruger make it difficult to spot game. Game-viewing is at its very best at the onset of a drought following several years of above-average rainfall. At this stage, game numbers have peaked and gather in areas surrounding the few remaining water sources. A prolonged drought, unfortunately, also guarantees a general decline in game numbers, although lion and other predators may temporarily thrive on easy pickings.

THE SUCCESSFUL GAME DRIVE

The unpredictability of game-viewing is probably what makes the experience so fascinating. That said, the most consistently productive times are early morning and late afternoon. Unfortunately, in the more popular camps, keen game-viewers will begin lining up at the gate (up